Wilkie Collins

Alicia Warlock, a Mystery

And other Stories

Wilkie Collins

Alicia Warlock, a Mystery
And other Stories

ISBN/EAN: 9783744749794

Printed in Europe, USA, Canada, Australia, Japan

Cover: Foto ©Andreas Hilbeck / pixelio.de

More available books at **www.hansebooks.com**

Faithfully yours
Wilkie Collins

ALICIA WARLOCK,

(*A MYSTERY,*)

AND

OTHER STORIES.

BY

WILKIE COLLINS.

AUTHOR OF "THE WOMAN IN WHITE," "NO NAME," "THE FROZEN DEEP,"
"THE LAW AND THE LADY," ETC.

BOSTON:

WILLIAM F. GILL & COMPANY,

309 WASHINGTON STREET.

1875.

[INTRODUCTORY NOTE. — The original version of this story was published, many years ago, in "Household Words." In the present version new characters and new incidents are introduced; and a new beginning and ending have been written. Indeed, the whole complexion of the narrative differs so essentially from the older and shorter version, as to justify me in believing that the reader will find in these pages what is, to all practical intents and purposes, a new story. — W. C.]

ROCKWELL & CHURCHILL,
Printers and Stereotypers, Boston.

ALICIA WARLOCK.

A MYSTERY.

PERSONS OF THE MYSTERY.

FRANCIS RAVEN.........................(Ostler)
MRS. RAVEN.........................(His Mother)
MRS. CHANCE......................:.......(His Aunt)
PERCY FAIRBANK } ..(His Master and Mistress)
MRS. FAIRBANK }
JOSEPH RIGOBERT........,..(His Fellow-servants).
ALICIA WARLOCK....................(His Wife)

PERIOD—THE PRESENT TIME.
SCENE—PARTLY IN ENGLAND, PARTLY IN FRANCE.

THE FIRST NARRATIVE.

INTRODUCTORY STATEMENT OF THE FACTS.
BY PERCY FAIRBANK.

I.

"Hullo, there! Ostler! Hullo-o-o!"

"My dear, why don't you look for the bell?"

"I *have* looked—there is no bell."

"And nobody in the yard. How very extraordinary! Call again, dear."

"Ostler! Hullo, there! Ostler r-r!"

My second call echoes through empty space, and rouses nobody — produces, in short, no visible result. I am at the end of my resources—I don't know what to say or what to do next. Here I stand in the solitary inn yard of a strange town, with two horses to hold and a lady to take care of. By way of adding to my responsibilities, it so happens that one of the horses is dead lame, and that the lady is my wife.

Who am I?—you will ask.

There is plenty of time to answer the question. Nothing happens; and nobody appears to receive us. Let me introduce myself and my wife.

I am Percy Fairbank, English gentleman, age (let us say) forty, no profession, moderate politics, middle height, fair complexion, easy character, plenty of money.

My wife is a French lady. She was Mlle. Clotilde Delorge, when I was first presented to her at her father's house in France. I fell in love with her; I really don't know why. It might have been because I was perfectly idle, and had nothing else to do at the time. Or it might have been because all my friends said she was the very last woman I ought to think of marrying. On the surface, I must own, there is nothing in common between Mrs. Fairbank and me. She is tall; she is dark; she is nervous, excitable, romantic; in all her opinions she proceeds to extremes. What could such a woman see in me? What could I see in her? I know no more than you do. In some mysterious manner, we exactly suit each other. We have been man and wife for ten years, and our only regret is that we have no children. I don't know what *you* may think; *I* call that (upon the whole) a happy marraige.

So much for ourselves. The next question is, What has brought us into the inn yard, and why am I obliged to turn groom, and hold the horses?

We live for the most part in France, at the country house in which my wife and I first met. Occasionally, by way of variety, we pay visits to my friends in England. We are paying one of those visits now. Our host is an old college friend of mine, possessed of a fine estate in Somersetshire, and we have arrived at his house—called Farleigh Hall—towards the close of the hunting season. On the day of which I am now writing —destined to be a memorable day in our calendar—the hounds meet at Farleigh Hall. Mrs Fairbank and I are mounted on two of the best horses in my friend's stables. We are quite unworthy of that distinction, for we know nothing, and care nothing, about hunting. On the other hand, we delight in riding, and we enjoy the breezy spring morning and the fair and fertile English landscape surrounding us on every side. While the hunt prospers we follow the hunt. But when 'a check occurs—when time passes and patience is sorely tried; when the bewildered dogs run hither and thither, and strong language falls from the lips of exasperated sportsmen—we fail to take any further interest in the proceedings. We turn our horses' heads in the direction of a grassy lane, delightfully shaded by trees. We trot merrily along the lane, and find ourselves on an open common. We gallop across the common and follow the windings of a second lane. We cross a brook, we pass through a village, we emerge into pastorial solitude among the hills. The horses toss their heads and neigh to each other, and enjoy it as much as we do. The hunt is forgotten. We are as happy as a couple of children; we are actually singing a French song when, in one moment, our merriment comes to an end. My wife's horse sets one of his fore-feet on a loose stone and stumbles. His rider's ready hand saves him from falling. But, at the first attempt he makes to go on, the sad truth shows itself—a tendon is strained; the horse is lame.

What is to be done? We are strangers in a lonely part of the country. Look where we may, we see no signs of a human habitation. There is nothing for it but to take the bridle-road up the hill, and try what we can discover on the other side. I transfer the saddles, and mount my wife on my own horse. He is not used to carry a lady; he misses the familiar pressure of a man's legs on either side of him; he fidgets and starts and kicks up the dust. I follow on foot, at a respectful distance from his heels, leading the lame horse. Is there a more miserable object on the face of creation than a lame horse? I have seen lame men and lame dogs who were cheerful creatures—but I never yet saw a lame horse who didn't look heartbroken over his own misfortune.

For half an hour my wife capers and curvets sideways along the bridle-road. I trudge on behind her; and the heartbroken horse halts behind *me*. Hard by the top of the hill, our melancholoy procession passes a Somersetshire peasant at work in a field. I summon the man to approach us; and the man looks at me stolidly, from the middle of the field, without stirring a step. I ask at the top of my voice how far it is to Farleigh Hall. The Somersetshire peasant answers at the top of *his* voice:

"Vourteen mile. Gi' oi a drap o' zyder.'"

I translate, for my wife's benefit, from the Somersetshire language into the English language. We are fourteen miles from Farleigh Hall, and our friend in the field desires to be rewarded, for giving us that information, with a drop of cider. There is the peasant, painted by himself. Quite a bit of character, my dear! Quite a bit of character!

Mrs. Fairbank doesn't view the study of agricultural human nature with my relish. Her fidgety horse will not allow her a moment's repose; she is beginning to lose her temper.

"We can't go fourteen miles in this way," she says. "Where is the nearest inn? Ask that brute in the field!"

I take a shilling from my pocket and hold it up in the sun. The shilling exercises magnetic virtues. The shilling draws the peasant slowly towards me from the middle of the field. I inform him that we want to put up the horses and to hire a carriage to take us back to Farleigh Hall. Where can we do that? The peasant answers, with his eye on the shilling:

"At Oonderbridge, to be zure. (At Underbridge, to be sure.)

"Is it far to Underbridge?"

The peasant repeats, "Var to Oonderbridge?"—and laughs at the question. "Hoo-hoo-hoo!" (Underbridge is evidently close by—if we could only find it.) "Will you show us the way, my man?" "Will you gi' oi a drap o' zyder?" I courteously bend my head, and point to the shilling. The agricultural intelligence exerts itself. The peasant joins our melancholy procession. My wife is a fine woman, but he never once looks at my wife—and, more extraordinary still, he never even looks at the horses. His eyes are with his mind—and his mind is on the shilling.

We reach the top of the hill—and, behold, on the other side, nestling in a valley, the shrine of our pilgrimage, the town of Underbridge. Here our guide claims his shilling, and leaves us to find out the inn for ourselves. I am constitutionally a polite man. I say "Good morning" at parting. The guide looks at me with the shilling between his teeth to make sure that it is a good one. "Marnin!" he says, savagely—and turns his back on us, as if we had offended him. A curious product, this, of the growth of civilization. If I didn't see a church spire at Underbridge, I might suppose that we had lost ourselves on a savage island.

II.

Arriving at the town, we have no difficulty in finding the inn. The town is composed of one desolate street, and midway in that street stands the inn—an ancient stone building sadly out of repair. The painting on the signboard is obliterated. The shutters over the long range of front windows are all closed. A cock and his hens are the only living creatures at the door. Plainly, this is one of the old inns of the stage-coach period, ruined by the railway. We pass through the open arched doorway, and find no one to welcome us. We advance into the stable-yard behind; I assist my wife to dismount—and there we are in the position already disclosed to view, at the opening of this narrative. No bell to ring. No human creature to answer when I call. I stand helpless, with the bridles of the horses in my hand. Mrs. Fairbank saunters gracefully down the length of the yard, and does—what all women do, when they find themselves in a strange place. She opens every door as she passes it and peeps in. On my side, I have just recovered my breath; I am on the point of shoutngi for the ostler for the third and last time, when I hear Mrs. Fairbank suddenly call to me.

"Percy, come here!"

Her voice is eager and agitated. She has opened a last door at the end of the yard, and has started back from some sight which has suddenly met her view. I hitch the horse's bridle on a rusty nail in the wall near me and join my wife. She has turned pale and catches me nervously by the arm.

"Good heavens!" she cries, "look at that!"

I look, and what do I see?

I see a dingy little stable, containing two stalls. In one stall, a horse is munching his corn. In the other, a man is lying asleep on the litter.

A worn, withered, woe-begone man in an ostler's dress. His hollow, wrinkled cheeks, his scanty, grizzled hair, his dry, yellow skin, tell their own tale of past sorrow or suffering. There is an ominous frown on his eye-brows—there is a painful nervous contraction on one side of his mouth. I hear him breathing convulsively when I first look in; he shudders and sighs in his sleep. It is not a pleasant sight to see, and I turn round instinctively to the bright sunlight in the yard. My wife turns me back again in the direction of the stable door.

"Wait!" she says. "Wait! He may do it again."

"Do what again?"

"He was talking in his sleep, Percy, when I first looked in. He was dreaming some dreadful dream. Hush! he's beginning again.

I look and listen. The man stirs on his miserable bed. The man speaks, in a quick, fierce whisper, through his clenched teeth. "Wake up! Wake up, there! Murder!"

There is an interval of silence. He moves one lean arm slowly until it rests over his throat; he shudders, and turns on his straw; he raises his arm from his throat, and feebly stretches it out; his hand clutches at the straw on the side towards which he has turned; he seems to fancy that he is grasping at the edge of something; I see his lips being to move again; I step softly into the stable; my wife follows me, with her hand fast clasped in mine. We both bend over him. He is talking once more in his sleep—strange talk, mad talk, this time.

"Light gray eyes" (we hear him say) "and a droop in the left eyelid—flaxen hair, with a gold-yellow streak in it—all right, mother! Fair white arms with a down on them—little, lady's hand, with a reddish look round the finger-nails—the knife—the cursed knife—first on one side, then on the other—aha, you she-devil! where is the knife?"

He stops and grows restless on a sudden. We see him writhing on the straw. He throws up both his hands and gasps hysterically for breath. His eyes open suddenly. For a moment they look at nothing, with a vacant glitter in them; then they close again in deeper sleep. Is he dreaming still? Yes; but the dream seems to have taken a new course. When he speaks next the tone is altered, the words are few, sadly and imploringly repeated over and over again: "Say you love me! I am so fond of you. Say you love me! Say you love me!" He sinks into deeper and deeper sleep, faintly repeating those words. They die away on his lips. He speaks no more.

By this time, Mrs. Fairbank has got over her terror. She is devoured with curiosity now. The miserable creature on the straw has appealed to the imaginative side of her character. Her illimitable appetite for romance hungers and thirsts for more. She shakes me impatiently by the arm. "Do you hear? There is a woman at the bottom of it, Percy! There is love and murder in it, Percy! Where are the people of the inn? Go into the yard and call to them again."

My wife belongs, on her mother's side, to the South of France. The South of France breeds fine women with hot tempers. I say no more. Married men will understand my position. Single men may need to be told that there are occasions when we must not only love and honor—we must also obey our wives.

I turn to the stable door to obey *my* wife, and find myself confronting a stranger who stands watching us. The stranger is a tiny, sleepy, rosy old man, with a vacant pudding-face, and a shining bald head. He wears drab breeches and gaiters, and a respectable square-tailed ancient black coat. I feel instinctively that here is the landlord of the inn.

"Good morning, sir," says the rosy old man. "I'm a little hard of hearing. Was it you that was a-calling just now in the yard?"

Before I can answer, my wife interposes. She insists (in a shrill voice, adapted to our host's hardness of hearing) on knowing who that unfortunate person is sleeping on the straw? "Where does he come from? Why does he say such dreadful things in his sleep? Is he married or single? Did he ever fall in love with a murderess? What sort of a looking woman was she? Did she really stab him or not? In short, dear Mr. Landlord, tell us the whole story!"

Dear Mr. Landlord waits drowsily until Mrs. Fairbank has quite done—then delivers himself of his reply, as follows:

"His name's Francis Raven. He's an Independent Methodist. He was forty-five year old last birthday. And he's my ostler. That's his story."

My wife's hot Southern temper finds its way to her foot, and expresses itself by a stamp on the stable-yard.

The landlord turns himself sleepily round, and looks at the horses. "A fine pair of horses, them two in the yard. Do you want to put 'em up in my stables?" I reply in the affirmative by a nod. The landlord, bent on making himself agreeable to my wife, addresses her once more. "I'm a-going to wake Francis Raven. He's an Independent Methodist. He was forty-five year old last birthday. And he's my ostler. That's his story."

Having issued this second edition of his interesting narrative, the landlord enters the stable. We follow him to see how he will wake Francis Raven, and what will happen upon that. The stable-broom stands in a corner; the landlord takes it—advances towards the sleeping ostler—and coolly stirs the man up with the broom as if he was a wild beast in a cage. Francis Raven starts to his feet with a cry of terror—looks at us wildly, with a horrid glare of suspicion in his eyes—recovers himself the next moment—and suddenly changes into a decent, quiet, respectable serving man.

"I beg your pardon, ma'am. I beg your pardon, sir."

The tone and manner in which he makes his apologies are both above his apparent station in life. I begin to catch the infection of Mrs. Fairbank's interest in this man. We both follow him out into the yard, to see what he will do with the horses. The manner in which he lifts the injured leg of the lame horse tells me at once that he understands his business. Quickly and quietly, he leads the animals into an empty stable; quickly and quietly, he gets a bucket of hot water, and puts the lame horse's leg into it. "The warm water will reduce the swelling, sir. I will bandage the leg afterwards." All that he does is done intelligently; all that he says, he says to the purpose. Nothing wild, nothing strange about him, now. Is this the same man whom we heard talking in his sleep? the same man who woke with that cry of terror and that horrid suspicion in his eyes? I determine to try him with one or two questions.

III.

"Not much to do here," I say to the ostler.

"Very little to do, sir," the ostler replies.

"Anybody staying in the house?"

"The house is quite empty, sir."

"I thought you were all dead. I could make nobody hear me."

"The landlord is very deaf, sir, and the waiter is out on an errand."

"Yes—and you were fast asleep in the stable. Do you often take a nap in the day-time?"

The worn face of the ostler faintly flushes. His eyes look away from my eyes for the first time. Mrs. Fairbank furtively pinches my arm. Are we on the eve of a discovery at last? I repeat my question. The man has no civil alternative but to give me an answer. The answer is given in these words:

"I was tired out, sir. You wouldn't have found me asleep in the day-time but for that."

"Tired out, eh? You had been hard at work, I suppose?"

"No, sir."

"What was it, then?"

He hesitates again, and answers unwillingly; "I was up all night."

"Up all night? Anything going on in the town?"

"Nothing going on, sir."

"Anybody ill?"

"Nobody ill, sir."

That reply is the last. Try as I may, I can extract nothing more from him. He turns away and busies himself in attending to the horse's leg. I leave the stable, to speak to the landlord about the carriage which is to take us back to Farleigh Hall. Mrs. Fairbank remains with the ostler, and favors me with a look at parting. The look says, plainly: "I mean to find out why he was up all night. Leave him to me."

The ordering of the carriage is easily accomplished. The inn possesses one horse and one chaise. The landlord has a story to tell of the horse, and a story to tell of the chaise. They resemble the story of Francis Raven—with this exception, that the horse and chaise belong to no religious persuasion. "The horse will be nine year old next birthday. I've had the shay for four and twenty year. Mr. Max of Underbridge, he bred the horse; and Mr. Pooley of Yeovil, he built the shay. It's my horse and my shay. And that's *their* story!" Having relieved his mind of these details, the landlord proceeds to put the harness on the horse. By way of assisting him, I drag the chaise into the yard. Just as our preparations are completed, Mrs. Fairbank appears. A moment or two later, the ostler follows her out. He has bandaged the horse's leg, and is now ready to drive us to Farleigh Hall.

I observe signs of agitation in his face and manner, which suggest that my wife has found her way into his confidence. I put the question to her privately in a corner of the yard. "Well? Have you found out why Francis Raven was up all night?"

Mrs. Fairbank has an eye to dramatic effect. Instead of answering plainly, Yes or No, she suspends the interest and excites the audience by putting a question on her side.

"What is the day of the month, dear?"

"The day of the month is the 1st of March.

"The 1st of March, Percy, is Francis Raven's birthday."

I try to look as if I was interested—and don't succeed.

"Francis was born," Mrs. Fairbank proceeds, gravely, "at 2 o'clock in the morning."

I begin to wonder whether my wife's intellect is going the way of the landlord's intellect. "Is that all?" I ask.

"It is not all," Mrs. Fairbank answers. "Francis Raven sits up on the morning of his birthday, because he is afraid to go to bed."

"And why is he afraid to go to bed?"

"Because he is in peril of his life."

"On his birthday?"

"On his birthday. At 2 o'clock in the morning. As regularly as the birthday comes round."

There she stops. Has she discovered no more than that? No more thus far. I begin to feel really interested by this time. I ask eagerly what it means? Mrs. Fairbank points mysteriously to the chaise—with Francis Raven (hitherto our ostler, now our coachman) waiting for us to get in. The chaise has a seat for two in front—and a seat for one be-hind. My wife casts another warning look at me, and places herself on the seat in front.

The necessary consequence of this arrangement is, that Mrs. Fairbank sits by the side of the driver, during a journey of two hours and more. Need I state the result? It would be an insult to your intelligence to state the result? Let me offer you my place in the chaise. And let Francis Raven tell his terrible story to you, as he told it to us, in his own words.

THE SECOND NARRATIVE.

THE OSTLER'S STORY. TOLD BY HIMSELF.

IV.

It is now ten years ago, since I got my first warning of the great trouble of my life, in the Vision of a Dream.

I shall be better able to tell you about it if you will please suppose yourselves to be drinking tea, along with us, in our little cottage in Cambridgeshire, ten years ago.

The time was the close of day, and there were three of us at the table, namely, my mother, myself, and my mother's sister, Mrs. Chance. These two were Scotchwomen by birth, and both were widows. There was no other resemblance between them, that I can call to mind. My mother had lived all her life in England, and had no more of the Scotch brogue on her tongue than I have. My Aunt Chance had never been out of Scotland until she came to keep house with my mother, after her husband's death. And when she opened her lips you heard broad Scotch, I can tell you, if ever you heard it yet.

As it fell out, there was a matter of some consequence in debate among us, that evening. It was this: Whether I should do well or not to take a long journey on foot, the next morning.

Now, the next morning happened to be the day before my birthday; and the purpose of the journey was to offer myself for a situation as groom, at a great house in the neighboring county to ours. The place was reported as likely to fall vacant in about three weeks' time. I was as well fitted to fill it as any other man. In the prosperous days of our family, my father had been manager of a training-stable; and he had kept me employed among the horses from my boyhood upward. Please to excuse my troubling you with these small matters. They all fit into my story farther on, as you will soon find out.

My poor mother was dead against my leaving home on the morrow.

"You can never walk all the way there and all the way back again by tomorrow night," she says. "The end of it will be that you will sleep away from home on your birthday. You have never done that yet, Francis, since your father's death. I don't like your doing it now. Wait a day longer, my son — only one day."

For my own part, I was weary of being idle; and I couldn't abide the notion of delay. Even one day might make all the difference. Some other man might take time by the forelock and get the place.

"Consider how long I have been out of work," I says—"and don't ask me to put off the journey. I won't fail you, mother. I'll get back by tomorrow night, if I have to pay my last sixpence for a lift in a cart."

My mother shook her head. "I don't like it, Francis—I don't like it!" There was no moving her from that view. We argued and argued, until we were both at a dead-lock. It ended in our agreeing to refer the difference between us to my mother's sister, Mrs. Chance.

While we were trying hard to convince each other, my Aunt Chance sat as dumb as a fish, stirring her tea and thinking her own thoughts. When we made our appeal to her, she seemed, as it were, to wake up. "Ye baith refer it to my puir judgment?" she says, in her broad Scotch. We both answered yes. Upon that my aunt Chance first cleared the tea-table, and then pulled out from the pocket of her gown a pack of cards.

Don't run away, if you please, with the notion that this was done lightly, with a view to amuse my mother and me. My Aunt Chance seriously believed that she could look into the future by telling fortunes on the cards. She did nothing herself without first consulting the cards; and she could give no more serious proof of her interest in my welfare than the proof which she was offering now. I don't say it profanely; I only mention the fact—the cards had, in some incomprehensible way, got themselves jumbled up together with her religious convictions. You meet with people nowadays who believe in spirits working by way of tables and chairs. On the same principle (if there is any principle in it) my Aunt Chance believed in Providence working by way of the cards.

"Whether you are right, Francis, or your mither—whether ye will do weel or ill, the morrow, to go or stay—the cairds will tell it. We are a' in the hands of Proavidence. The cairds will tell it."

Hearing this, my mother turned her head aside, with something of a sour look in her face. Her sister's notions about the cards were little better than flat blasphemy, to her mind. But she kept her opinion to herself. My Aunt Chance, to own the truth, had inherited, through her late husband, a pension of £30 a year. This was an important contribution to our housekeeping—and we poor relations were bound to treat her with a certain respect. As for myself—if my poor father never did anything else for me before he fell into difficulties—he gave me a good education, and raised me (thank God) above superstitions of all sorts. However, a very little amused me in those days; and I waited to have my fortune told, as patiently as if I believed in it too!

My aunt began her hocus-pocus by throwing out all the cards in the pack under seven. She shuffled the rest, with her left hand, for luck; and then she gave them to me to cut. "Wi' yer left hand, Francie. Mind that! Pet yer trust in Proavidence—but dinna forget that yer luck's in yer left hand!" A long and roundabout shifting of the cards followed, reducing them in number, until there were just fifteen of them left, laid out neatly before my aunt in a half circle. The card which happened to lay outermost, at the right-hand end of the circle, was, according to rule in such cases, the card chosen to represent me. By way of being appropriate to my situation as a poor groom out of work, the card was—the King of Diamonds.

"I tak' up the King o' Diamants," says my aunt. "I count seven cairds fra' right to left; and I humbly ask a blessing on what follows." My aunt shut her eyes as if she was saying grace before meat, and held up to me the seventh card. I called the seventh card—the Queen of Spades. My aunt opened her eyes again in a hurry, and cast a sly look my way. "The Queen o' Spades means a dairk woman. Ye'll be thinking, in secret, Francie, of a dairk woman?"

When a man has been out of place for more than three months, his mind isn't troubled much with thinking of women—light or dark. I was thinking of the groom's place at the great house; and I tried to say so. My Aunt Chance wouldn't listen. She treated my interruption with contempt. "Hoot-toot! there's the caird in your hand! If ye're no thinking of her, today, ye'll be thinking of her, tomorrow. Where's the harm of thinking of a dairk woman? I was aince a dairk woman myself, before my hair was gray. Haud yer peace, Francie—and watch the cairds."

I watched the cards as I was told. There were seven left on the table. My aunt removed two from one end of the row, and two from the other—and desired me to call the two outermost of the three cards now left on the table. I called the Ace of Clubs and the Ten of Diamonds. My Aunt Chance lifted her eyes to the ceiling with a look of devout gratitude which sorely tried my mother's patience. The Ace of Clubs and the Ten of Diamonds, taken together, signified—first, good news (evidently the news of the groom's place!) secondly, a journey that lay before me (pointing plainly to my journey, tomorrow!); thirdly and lastly, a sum of money (probably the groom's wages!) waiting to find its way into my pockets. Having told my fortune in these encouraging terms, my aunt declined to carry the experiment any farther. "Eh, lad! it's a clean tempting of Proavidence to ask mair o' the cairds then the cairds have tauld us noo. Gae yer ways tomorrow to the great hoose."

A dairk woman will meet ye at the gate; and she'll have a hand in getting ye the groom's place, wi' a' the graitifications and pairquisites appertaining to the same. And, mebbe, when yer poaket's full o' money, ye'll no' be forgettin yer Aunt Chance, maintaining her ain unbleemished widowhood — wi' Proavidence assistin'—on thratty[punds a year!"

I promised to remember my Aunt Chance (who had the defect, by way, of being a terribly greedy person after money) on the next happy occasion when my poor empty pockets were to be filled at last. This done, I looked at my mother. She had agreed to take her sister for umpire between us—and her sister had given it in my favor. She raised no more objections. Silently, she got on her feet and kissed me and sighed bitterly—and so left the room. My Aunt Chance shook her head. "I doubt, Francie, yer puir mither has but a heathen notion of the vairtue of the cairds!"

By daylight, the next morning, I set forth on my journey. I looked back at the cottage as I opened the garden gate. At one window, was my mother, with her handkerchief to her eyes. At the other, stood my Aunt Chance, holding up the Queen of Spades by way of encouraging me at starting. I waved my hand to both of them in token of farewell, and stepped out briskly into the road. It was then the last day of February. Be pleased to remember, in connection with this, that the first of March was the day, and 2 o'clock in the morning the hour of my birth.

V.

Now you know how I came to leave home. The next thing to tell is what happened on the journey.

I reached the great house in reasonably good time considering the distance. At the very first trial of it the prophecy of the cards turned out to be wrong. The person who met me at the lodge gate was not a dark woman; in fact, not a woman at all, but a boy. He directed me on the way to the servants' offices, and there, again, the cards were all wrong. I encountered not one woman, but three, and not one of the three was, dark. I have stated that I am not superstitious and I have told the truth. But I must own that I did feel a certain fluttering at the heart when I made my bow to the steward and told him what business had brought me to the house. His answer completed the discomfiture of Aunt Chance's fortune-telling. My ill-luck still pursued me. That very morning, another man had applied for the groom's place, and had got it.

I swallowed my disappointment as well as I could—and thanked the steward—and went to the inn in the village to get the rest and food which I sorely needed by this time.

Before starting on my homeward walk, I made some inquiries at the inn, and found out that I might save a few miles on my return, by following a new road. Furnished with full instructions, several times repeated, as to the various turnings I was to take, I set forth, and walked on till the evening with only one stoppage for bread and cheese. Just as it was getting towards dark, the rain came on and the wind began to rise; and I found myself, to make matters worse, in a part of the country with which I was entirely unacquainted, though I guessed myself to be some fifteen miles from home. The first house I found to inquire at, was a lonely roadside inn, standing on the outskirts of a thick wood. Solitary as the place looked, it was welcome to a lost man who was also hungry, thirsty, footsore and wet. The landlord was civil and respectable-looking, and the price he asked for a bed was resonable enough. I was grieved to disappoint my mother. But there was no conveyance to be had, and I could go no farther afoot that night. My wearness fairly forced me to stop at the inn.

I may say for myself that I am a temperate man. My supper simply consisted of some rashers of bacon, a slice of home-made bread, and a pint of ale. I did not go to bed immediately after this moderate meal, but sat up with the landlord, talking about my bad prospects and my long run of ill-luck, and diverging from these topics to the subjects of horse-flesh and racing. Nothing was said either by myself, my host, or the few laborers who strayed into the tap-room, which could, in the slightest degree, excite my mind or set my fancy—which is only a small fancy at the best of time—playing tricks with my common sense.

At a little after 11, the house was closed. I went round with the landlord and held the candle while the doors and lower windows were being secured. I noticed, with surprise, the strength of the bolts, bars and iron-sheathed shutters.

"You see, we are rather lonely here," says the landlord. "We never have had any attempts to break in yet, but it's always as well to be on the safe side. When nobody is sleeping here I am the only man in the house. My wife and daughter are timid, and the servant girl takes after her missuses. Another glass of ale before you turn in? No! Well, how such a sober man as you comes to be out of place is more than I can understand, for one. Here's where you are to sleep. You're the only lodger, tonight, and I think you'll say my missus has done her best to make you comfortable. You're quite sure you won't have another glass of ale? Very well. Good night.

It was half-past 11 by the clock in the passage as we went up-stairs to the bedroom. The window looked out on the road at the back of the house.

I locked my door, set my candle on the chest of drawers, and wearily got me ready for bed. The bleak wind was still blowing, and the solemn surging moan of it in the wood was very dreary to hear through the night silence. I felt strangely wakeful. I resolved to keep the candle alight until I began to grow sleepy. The truth is, I was not quite myself. I was depressed in mind by my disappointment of the morning; and I was worn out in body by my long walk. Between the two, I own I couldn't face the prospect of lying awake in the dark-ness, listening to the dismal moan of the wind in the wood.

Sleep stole on me before I was aware of it; my eyes closed, and I fell off to rest, without having so much as thought of extinguishing the candle.

The next thing that I remember was a faint shivering that ran through me from head to foot, and a dreadful sink-ing pain at my heart, such as I had never felt before. The shivering only dis-turbed my slumbers—the pain woke me instantly. In one moment I passed from a state of sleep to a state of wakeful-ness—my eyes wide open—my mind clear on a sudden as if by a miracle.

The candle had burnt down nearly to the last morsel of tallow, but the un-snuffed wick had just fallen off, and the light was, for the moment, fair and full.

Between the foot of the bed and the closed door, I saw a person in my room. The person was a woman, standing looking at me, with a knife in her hand.

It does no credit to my courage to confess it—but the truth is the truth. I was struck speechless with terror. There I lay with my eyes on the woman; there the woman stood (with her knife in her hand) with *her* eyes on *me*.

She said not a word as we stared each other in the face; but she moved after a little—moved slowly toward the left-hand side of the bed.

The light fell full on her face. A fair, fine woman, with yellowish flaxen hair, and light gray eyes with a droop in the left eyelid. I noticed these things and fixed them in my mind, before she was quite round at the side of the bed. Without saying a word; without any change in the stony stillness of her face; without any noise following her footfall, she came closer and closer; stopped at the bed-head, and lifted the knife to stab me. I laid my arm over my throat to save it; but, as I saw the blow coming, I threw my hand across the bed to the right side, and jerked my body over that way, just as the knife came down like lightning on the mattress within a hairs-breadth of my shoulder.

VI.

My eyes fixed on her arm and her hand—she gave me time to look at them as she slowly drew her knife out of the bed. A white, well-shaped arm, with a pretty down lying lightly over the fair skin; a delicate lady's hand, with a pink flush round the finger-nails.

She drew the knife out, and passed back again slowly to the foot of the bed;

she stopped there for a moment, looking at me; then she came on without saying a word, without any change in the stony stillness of her face, without any noise following her footfall—came on to the side of the bed where I now lay.

Getting near me, she lifted the knife again, and I drew myself away to the left side. She struck, as before, right into the mattress, with a swift downward action of her arm; and she missed me as before by a hairs-breadth. This time my eyes wandered from *her* to the knife. It was like the large clasp-knives which laboring men use to cut their bread and bacon with. Her delicate little fingers did not hide more than two-thirds of the handle; I noticed that it was made of buckhorn, clean and shining as the blade was, and looking like new.

For the second time she drew the knife out of the bed, and suddenly hid it away in the wide sleeve of her gown. That done, she stopped by the bedside, watching me. For an instant I saw her standing in that position—then the wick of the spent candle fell over into the socket. The flame dwindled to a little blue point, and the room grew dark.

A moment, or less, if possible, passed so—and then the wick flamed up, smokily, for the last time. My eyes were still looking for her over the right-hand side of the bed when the last flash of light came. Look as I might, I could see nothing. The woman with the knife was gone.

I began to get back to myself again. I could feel my heart beating; I could hear the woful moaning of the wind in the wood; I could leap up in bed, and give the alarm before she escaped from the house. "Murder! Wake up there! Murder!"

Nobody answered to the alarm. I rose and groped my way through the darkness to the door of the room. By that way she must have got in. By that way she must have gone out.

The door of the room was fast locked, exactly as I had left it on going to bed! I looked at the window. The window was fast locked, too.

For a moment I stood lost in amazement. Then, hearing a voice outside, I opened the door. There was the landlord, coming toward me along the passage, with his burning candle in one hand, and his gun in the other.

"What is it?" he says, looking at me in no very friendly way.

I could only answer him in a whisper. "A woman, with a knife in her hand. In my room. A fair, yellow-haired woman. She jobbed at me with the knife, twice over."

He lifted his candle, and looked at me steadily from head to foot.

"She seems to have missed you twice over."

"I dodged the knife as it came down. It struck the bed each time. Go in and see."

The landlord took his candle into the bed-room immediately. In less than a minute he came out again into the passage in a violent passion.

"The devil fly away with you and your woman with the knife! There isn't a mark in the bed-clothes anywhere. What do you mean by coming into a man's place and frightening his family out of their wits by a dream?"

A dream? The woman who had tried to stab me, not a living human being like myself? I began to shake and shiver. The horrors got hold of me at the bare thought of it.

"I'll leave the house," I said. "Bet-ter out on the road in the rain and dark than back again in that room, after what I've seen in it. Lend me the light to get my clothes by, and tell me what I'm to pay."

The landlord led the way back with his light into the bed-room. "Pay?" says he. "You'll find your score on the slate when you go down-stairs. I wouldn't have taken you in for all the money you've got about you, if I had known your dreaming, screeching ways beforehand. Look at the bed. Where's the cut of a knife in it? Look at the window—is the lock bursted? Look at the door (which I heard you fasten yourself)—is it broke in? A murdering woman with a knife in my house! You ought to be ashamed of yourself!"

My eyes followed his hand as it pointed first to the bed—then to the window—then to the door. There was no gainsaying it. The bed sheet was as sound as on the day it was made. The window was fast. The door hung on its hinges as steady as ever. I huddled my clothes on without speaking. We went down stairs together. I looked at the clock in the bar room. The time was twenty minutes past two in the morning. I paid my bill; and the landlord let me out. The rain had ceased; but the night was dark, and the wind was bleaker than ever. Little did the darkness, or the cold, or the doubt about the way home matter to *me*. My mind was away from all these things. My mind was fixed on the vision in the bed-room. What had I seen trying to murder me? The creature of a dream? Or that other creature from the world beyond the grave, whom men call ghost? I could make nothing of it as I walked along in the night. I had made nothing of it by mid-day—when I stood at last, after many times missing my road, on the doorstep of home.

VII.

My mother came out alone to welcome me back. There were no secrets between us two. I told her all that had happened — just as I have told it to you.

She kept silence till I had done. And then she put a question to me.

"What time was it, Francis, when you saw the woman in your dream?"

I had looked at the clock when I left the inn, and had noticed that the hands pointed to twenty minutes past two. Allowing for the time consumed in speaking to the landlord, and in getting on my clothes, I answered that I must first have seen the woman at two o'clock in the morning. In other words, I had not only seen her on my birthday — but at the hour of my birth.

My mother still kept silence. Lost in her own thoughts, she took me by the hand, and led me into the parlor. Her writing desk was on the table by the fire-place. She opened it, and signed to me to take a chair by her side.

"My son! your memory is a bad one — and mine is fast failing me. Tell me again what the woman looked like. I want her to be as well-known to both of us, years hence, as she is now."

I obeyed; wondering what strange fancy might be working in her mind. I spoke; and she wrote the words as they fell from my lips :

"Light gray eyes, with a droop in the left eyelid. Flaxen hair, with a gold-yellow streak in it. White arms, with a down upon them. Little, lady's hands, with a rosy-red look about the finger-nails."

"Did you notice how she was dressed Francis?"

"No, mother."

"Did you notice the knife?"

"Yes. A large clasp-knife, with a buck-horn handle as good as new."

My mother added the description of the knife. Also the year, month, day of the week, and hour of the day when the dream-woman appeared to me at the inn. That done, she locked up the paper in her desk.

"Not a word, Francis, to your aunt. Not a word to any living soul. Keep your Dream a secret between you and me."

The weeks passed, and the months passed. My mother never returned to the subject again. As for me, time which wears out all things, wore out my remembrance of the Dream. Little by little, the image of the Woman grew dimmer and dimmer. Little by little, she faded out of my mind.

VIII.

The story of the warning is now told. Judge for yourselves if it was a true warning or a false, when you hear what happened to me on my next birthday.

In the summer time of the year, the Wheel of Fortune turned the right way for me at last. I was smoking my pipe one day, near an old stone-quarry at the entrance to our village, when a carriage accident happened, which gave a new turn, as it were, to my lot in life. It was an accident of the commonest kind—not worth mentioning at any length. A lady driving herself; a runaway horse; a cowardly man servant in attendance, frightened out of his wits; and the stone-quarry too near to be agreeable — that is what I saw, all in a few moments, between two whiffs of my pipe. I stopped the horse at the edge of the quarry, and got myself a little hurt by the shaft of the chaise. But that didn't matter. The lady declared I had saved her life; and her husband, coming with her to our cottage, the next day, took me into his service then and there. The lady happened to be of a dark complexion; and it may amuse you to hear that my Aunt Chance instantly pitched on that circumstance as a means of saving the credit of the cards. Here was the promise of the Queen of Spades performed to the very letter, by means of "a dark woman," just as my aunt had told me! "In the time to come, Francie, beware o' pettin' yer ain blinded intairpretation on the cairds. Ye're ower ready, I trow, to murmur under dispensations of proavidence that ye canna fathom — like the Eesraelites of auld. I'll say nae mair to ye. Mebbe when the money's powering into yer poackets, ye'll no forget yer Aunt Chance, left like a sparrow on the housetop, wi' a sma' annuitee o' thratty punds a year."

I remained in my situation (at the West-end of London) until the spring of the New Year.

About that time, my master's health failed; the doctors ordered him away to foreign parts, and the establishment was broken up. But the turn in my luck still held good. When I left my place, I left it — thanks to the generosity of my kind master — with a yearly allowance granted to me, in remembrance of the day when I had saved my mistress's life. For the future I could go back to service or not as I pleased; my little income was enough to support my mother and myself.

My master and mistress left England towards the end of February. Certain matters of business to do for them detained me in London until the last day of the month. I was only able to leave for our village by the evening train, to keep my birthday with my mother as usual. It was bed-time when I got to the cottage; and I was sorry to find that she was far from well. To make matters worse, she had finished her bottle of medicine on the previous day, and had omitted to get it replenished as the doctor had strictly directed. He dispensed his own medicines, and I offered to go and knock him up. She refused to let me do this; and after giving me my supper, sent me away to my bed.

I fell asleep for a little, and woke again. My mother's bed chamber was next to mine. I heard my Aunt Chance's heavy footsteps going to and fro in the room, and suspecting something wrong, knocked at the door. My mother's pains had returned upon her; there was a serious necessity for relieving her sufferings as speedly as possible. I put on my clothes, and ran off with the medicine-bottle in my hand, to the other end of the village where the doctor lived. The church-clock chimed the quarter to two on my birthday just as I reached his house. One ring at the night-bell brought him to his bed-room window to speak to me. He told me to wait, and he would let me in at the surgery door. I noticed, while I was waiting, that the night was wonderfully fair and warm for the time of the year. The old stone-quarry where the carriage accident had happened was within view. The moon in the clear heavens lit it up almost as bright as day.

In a minute or two, the doctor let me into the surgery. I closed the door, noticing that he had left his room very lightly clad. He kindly pardoned my mother's neglect of his directions, and set to work at once at compounding the medicine. We were both intent on the bottle; he filling it and I holding the light—when we heard the surgery door suddenly opened from the street.

IX.

Who could possibly be up and about in our quiet village at that dark hour of the morning?

The person who had opened the door appeared within range of the light of the candle. To complete our amazement, the person proved to be a woman! She walked up to the counter, and standing side-by-side with me, lifted her veil. At the moment when she showed her face, I heard the church clock strike two. She was a stranger to me, and a stranger to the doctor. She was also, beyond all comparison, the most beautiful woman I have ever seen in my life.

"I saw the light under the door," she said. "I want some medicine."

She spoke quite composedly—as if there was nothing at all extraordinary in her being out in the village at two in the morning, and following me into the surgery to ask for medicine! The doctor stared at her as if he suspected his own eyes of deceiving him. "Who are you?" he asked. "How do you come to be wandering about at this time in the morning?"

She paid no heed to his questions. She only told him in the coolest manner what she wanted.

"I have got a bad toothache. I want a bottle of laudanum."

The doctor recovered himself when she asked for the laudanum.

He was on his own ground as it were when it came to a matter of laudanum, and he spoke to her, smartly enough this time.

"Oh, you have got the toothache, have you? Let me look at the tooth."

She shook her head, and laid a two-shilling piece on the counter.

"I won't trouble you to look at the tooth," she said. "There is the money. Let 'me have the laudanum, if you please."

The doctor put the two-shilling piece back again in her hand.

"I don't sell laudanum to strangers," he answered. "If you are in any distress of body or mind, that is another matter. I shall be glad to help you."

She put the money back in her pocket. "You can't help me," she said, as quietly as ever. "Good morning."

With that, she opened the surgery door to go out again into the street.

So far, I had not spoken a word on my side. I had stood with the candle in my hand (not knowing I was holding it)— with my eyes fixed on her—like a man bewitched. Her looks betrayed, even more plainly than her words, her resolution in one way or another, to destroy herself. When she opened the door, in my alarm at what might happen I found the use of my tongue.

"Stop!" I cried out. "Wait for me. I want to speak to you before you go away."

She lifted her eyebrows with a look of careless surprise, and a mocking smile on her lips.

"What can you have to say to me?" She stopped, and laughed to herself. "Why not?" she says. "I have got nothing to do, and nowhere to go." She turned back a step, and nodded to me. "You're a strange man—I think I'll humor you—I'll wait outside." The door of the surgery closed on her. She was gone.

I am ashamed to own what happened next. The only excuse for me is that I was really and truly a man bewitched.

I turned me round to follow her out, without once thinking of my mother. The doctor stopped me.

"Don't forget the medicine," he said. "And, if you will take my advice, don't trouble yourself about that woman. Rouse up the constable. It's his business to look after her—not yours."

I held out my hand for the medicine in silence; I was afraid I should fail in respect if I trusted myself to answer him. He must have seen, as I saw, that she wanted the laudanum to poison herself. He had, to my mind, taken a very heartless view of the matter. I just thanked him when he gave me the medicine—and went out.

She was waiting for me as she had promised; walking slowly to and fro, a tall, graceful, solitary figure in the bright moonbeams. They shed over her fair complexion, her bright golden hair, her large gray eyes, just the light that suited them best. She looked hardly mortal, when she first turned to speak of me.

"Well?" she said. "And what do you want?"

In spite of my pride, or my shyness, or my better sense—whichever it might be—all my heart went out to her in a moment. I caught hold of her by the hands, and owned what was in my thoughts, as freely as if I had known her for half a lifetime.

"You mean to destroy yourself," I said. "and I mean to prevent you from doing it. If I follow you about all night, I'll prevent you from doing it."

She laughed. "You saw yourself that he wouldn't sell me the laudanum. Do you really care whether I live or die?" She squeezed my hands gently as she put the question; her eyes searched mine with a languid lingering look in

them that ran through me like fire. My voice died away on my lips; I couldn't answer her.

She understood, without my answering. "You have given me a fancy for living, by speaking kindly to me," she said. "Kindness has a wonderful effect on women and dogs and other domestic animals. It is only men who are superior to kindness. Make your mind easy —I promise to take as much care of myself as if I was the happiest woman living! Don't let me keep you here, out of your bed. Which way are you going?"

Miserable wretch that I was, I had again forgotten my mother—with the medicine in my hand!

"I am going home," I said. "Where are you staying? At the inn?"

She laughed her bitter laugh, and pointed to the stone-quarry. "There is my inn for to-night," she said. "When I got tired of walking about, I rested there."

We walked on together, on my way home. I took the liberty of asking if she had any friends.

"I thought I had one friend left," she said, "or you would never have met me in this place. It turns out I was wrong. My friend's door was closed in my face some hours since; my friend's servant's threatened me with the police. I had nowhere else to go, after trying my luck in your neighborhood; and nothing left but my two-shilling piece and these rags on my back. What respectable innkeeper would take me into his house? I walked about, wondering how I could find my way out of the world—without disfiguring myself, and without suffering much pain. You have no river in these parts. I didn't see my way out of the world, till I heard you ringing at the doctor's house. I got a glimpse at the bottles in the surgery, when he let you in--and I thought of the laudanum directly. What were you doing there? Who is that medicine for? Your wife?"

"I am not married."

She laughed again. "Not married! If I was a little better dressed there might a chance for ME. Where do you live? Here?"

We had arrived, by this time, at my my mother's door. She held out her hand to say good-by. Houseless and homeless as she was, she never asked me to give her a shelter for the night. It was *my* proposal that she should rest under my roof — unknown to my mother and my aunt. Our kitchen was built out at the back of the cottage; she might remain there unseen and unheard until the household was astir in the morning. I led her into the kitchen, and set a chair for her by the dying embers of the fire. I dare say I was to blame — shamefully to blame, if you like. I only wonder what *you* would have done in my place. On your word of honor as a man, would *you* have let that beautiful creature wander back to the shelter of the stone-quarry like a stray dog? God help the woman who is foolish enough to trust and love you — if you would have done that.

I left her by the fire, and went to my mother's room.

X.

If you have ever felt the heart-ache, you will know what I suffered in secret when my mother took my hand, and said, "I am sorry, Francis, that your night's rest has been disturbed through *me*." I gave her the medicine; and I waited by her till the pains abated. My Aunt Chance went back to her bed; and

my mother and I were left alone. I noticed that her writing desk, moved from its customary place, was on the bed by her side. She saw me looking at it. "This is your birthday, Francis," she said. "Have you anything to tell me?" I had so completely forgotten my Dream, that I had no notion of what was passing in her mind when she said those words. For a moment there was a guilty fear in me that she suspected something, I turned away my face and said, "No, mother, I have nothing to tell." She signed to me to stoop down over the pillow and kiss her. "God bless you, my love," she said, "and many happy returns of the day." She patted my hand, and closed her weary eyes, and, little by little, fell off peaceably into sleep.

I stole down stairs again. I think the good influence of my mother must have followed me down. At any rate, this is true: I stopped with my hand on the closed kitchen door, and said to myself, "Suppose I leave the house, and leave the village, without seeing her or speaking to her more?"

Should I really have fled from temptation in this way, if I had been left to myself to decide? Who can tell? As things were, I was not left to decide. While my doubt was in my mind, she heard me, and opened the kitchen door. My eyes and her eyes met. That ended it.

We were together, unsuspected and undisturbed, for the next two hours. Time enough for her to reveal the secret of her wasted life. Time enough for her to take possession of me as her own, to do with me as she liked. It is needless to dwell here on the misfortunes which had brought her low; they are misfortunes too common to interest anybody. Her name was Alicia Warlock. · She had been born and bred a lady. She had lost her station, her character, and her friends. Virtue shuddered at the sight of her: and Vice had got her for the rest of her days. Shocking, and common, as I told you. It made no difference to *me*. I have said it already —I say it again —I was a man bewitched. Is there anything so very wonderful in that? Just remember who I was. Among the honest women in my own station in life, where could I have found the like of *her*? Could *they* walk as she walked? and look as she looked? When *they* gave me a kiss, did their lips linger over it as hers did? Had *they* her skin, her laugh, her foot, her hand, her touch? *She* never had a speck of dirt on her. I tell you her flesh was a perfume. When she embraced me, her arms folded round me like the wings of angels; and her smile covered me softly with its light like the sun in Heaven. I leave you to laugh at me, or to cry over me, just as your temper may incline. I am not trying to excuse myself—I am trying to explain. You are gentlefolks; what dazzled and maddened *me*, is every-day experience to *you*. Fallen or not, angel or devil, it came to this—she was a lady, and I was a groom.

Before the house was a stir, I got her away (by the workmen's train) to a large manufacturing town in our parts. Here —with my savings in money to help her —she could get her outfit of decent clothes, and her lodging among strangers who asked no questions so long as they were paid. Here —now on one pretence and now on another —I could visit her, and we could both plan together what our future lives were to be. I need not tell you that I stood pledged to make her my wife. A man in my

station always marries a woman of her sort.

Do you wonder if I was happy at this time? I should have been perfectly happy, but for one little drawback. It was this: I was never quite at my ease in the presence of my promised wife.

I don't mean that I was shy with her or suspicious of her, or ashamed of her. The uneasiness I am speaking of was caused by a faint doubt in my mind, whether I had not seen her somewhere, before the morning when we met at the doctor's house. Over and over again, I found myself wondering whether her face did not remind me of some other face —what other I never could tell. This strange feeling, this one question that could never be answered, vexed me to a degree that you would hardly credit. It came between us at the strangest times—oftenest, however, at night, when the candles were lit. You have known what it is to try and remember a forgotten name —and to fail, search as you may, to find it in your mind. That was my case. I failed to find my lost face, just as you failed to find your lost name.

In three weeks, we had talked matters over, and had arranged how I was to make a clean breast of it at home. By Alicia's advice, I was to describe her as having been one of my fellow-servants, during the time when I was employed under my kind master and mistress in London. There was no fear now of my mother taking any harm from the shock of a great surprise. Her health had improved during the three weeks' interval. On the first evening when she was able to take her old place at tea-time, I summoned my courage, and told her I was going to be married. The poor soul flung her arms round my neck, and burst out crying for joy. "Oh, Francis!" she says, "I am so glad you will have somebody to comfort you and care for you when I am gone!" As for my Aunt Chance, you can anticipate what *she* did, without being told. Ah me! If there had really been any prophetic virtue in the cards, what a terrible warning they might have given us that night!

It was arranged that I was to bring my promised wife to dinner at the cottage, the next day.

XI.

I own I was proud of Alicia when I led her into our little parlor at the appointed time. She had never, to my mind, looked so beautiful as she looked that day. I never noticed any other woman's dress; I noticed hers as carefully as if I had been a woman myself! She wore a black silk gown, with plain collar and cuffs and a modest lavender-colored bonnet, with one white rose in it placed at the side. My mother dressed in her Sunday best, rose up, all in a flutter, to welcome her daughter-in-law that was to be. She walked forward a few steps, half smiling, half in tears — she looked Alicia full in the face — and suddenly stood still. Her cheeks turned white in an instant; her eyes stared in horror; her hands dropped helplessly at her sides. She staggered back — and fell into the arms of my aunt, standing behind her. It was no swoon; she kept her senses. Her eyes turned slowly from Alicia to me. "Francis," she said, 'does that woman's face remind you of nothing?"

Before I could answer, she pointed to her writing desk on the table at the fireside. "Bring it!" she cried, "Bring it!"

At the same moment, I felt Alicia's hand laid on my shoulder, and saw Alicia's face red with anger — and no wonder!

"What does this mean?" she asked. "Does your mother want to insult me?"

I said a few words to quiet her, what they were I don't remember — I was so confused and astonished at the time. Before I had done, I heard my mother behind me.

My aunt had fetched her desk. She had opened it; she had taken a paper from it. Step by step, helping herself along by the wall, she came nearer and nearer — with the paper in her had. She looked at the paper — she looked in Alicia's face — she lifted the long, loose sleeve of her gown — and examined her hand and arm. I saw fear suddenly take the place of anger in Alicia's eyes. She shook herself free of my mother's grasp. "Mad!" she said to herself, "and Francis never told me." With these words she ran out of the room.

I was hastening out after her, when my mother signed me to stop. She read the words written on the paper. While they fell slowly, one by one, from her lips, she pointed towards the open door.

"Light gray eyes, with a droop in the left eyelid. Flaxen hair, with a gold-yellow streak in it. White arms, with a down upon them. Little, lady's hand, with a rosy-red look about the finger-nails. The Dream-Woman, Francis! The Dream-Woman!"

Something darkened the parlor window, as those words were spoken. I looked sidelong at the shadow. Alicia Warlock had come back! She was peering in at us over the low window-blind. There was the fatal face which had first looked at me in the bed-room of the lonely inn! There, resting on the window-blind, was the lovely little hand which had held the murderous knife. I *had* seen her before we met in the village. The Dream-Woman! The Dream-Woman!

XI.

I expect nobody to approve of what I have next to tell of myself.

In three weeks from the day when my mother had identified her with the Woman of the Dream, I took Alicia Warlock to Church, and made her my wife. I was a man bewitched. Again and again I say it, I was a man bewitched!

During the interval before my marriage, our little household at the cottage was broken up. My mother and my aunt quarrelled. My mother, believing in the Dream, entreated me to break off my engagement. My aunt, believing in the cards, urged me to marry.

This difference of opinion produced a dispute between them, in the course of which my Aunt Chance—quite unconscious of having any superstitious feelings of her own—actually set out the cards which prophesied happiness to me in my married life, and asked my mother whether anybody but "a blinded heathen could be fule enough after seeing those cairds to believe in a dream!" This was, naturally, too much for my mother's patience; hard words followed on either side; Mrs. Chance returned in dudgeon to her friends in Scotland. She left me a written statement of my future prospects, as revealed by the cards— and with it an address at which a Post Office order would reach her. "The day was no that far off," she remarked, "when Francie might remember what he owed to his Aunt Chance, maintaining her ain unbleem-ished widowhood on thratty punds a year."

Having refused to give her sanction to my marriage, my mother also refused to be present at the wedding, or to visit Alicia afterwards. There was no anger at the bottom of this conduct on her part. Believing as she did in the Dream, she was simply in mortal fear of my wife. I understood this—and I made allowances for her. Not a cross word passed between us. My one happy remembrance now—though I did disobey her in the matter of my marriage—is this: I loved and respected my good mother to the last.

As for my wife, she expressed no regret at the estrangement between her mother-in-law and herself. By common consent, we never spoke on that subject. We settled in the manufacturing town which I have already mentioned; and we kept a lodging house. My kind master, at my request, granted me a lump sum in place of my annuity. This put us into a good house, decently furnished. For a while, things went well enough. I may describe myself at this time of my life as a happy man.

My misfortunes began with a return of the complaint from which my mother had already suffered. The doctor confessed, when I asked him the question, that there was danger to be dreaded, this time. Naturally, after hearing this, I was a good deal away at the cottage. Naturally also, I left the business of looking after our house in my absence, to my wife. Little by little, I found her beginning to alter towards me. While my back was turned, she formed acquaintances with people of the doubtful and dissipated sort. One day, I observed something in her manner which forced the suspicion on me that she had been drinking. Before the week was out, my suspicion was a certainty. From keeping company with drunkards, she had grown to be a drunkard herself.

I did all a man could do to reclaim her. Quite useless! She had never really returned the love I felt for her; I had no influence; I could do nothing. My mother, hearing of this last worst trouble, resolved to try what her influence could do. Ill as she was, I found her one day dressed to go out.

"I am not long for this world, Francis," she said. "I shall not feel easy on my death-bed, unless I have done my best to the last to make you happy. I mean to put my own fears and my own feelings out of the question, and to go with you to your wife, and try what I can do to reclaim her. Take me home with you, Francis. Let me do all I can to help my son, before it's too late."

How could I disobey her? We took the railway to the town; it was only half an hour's ride. By one o'clock in the afternoon we reached my house. It was our dinner hour, and Alicia was in the kitchen. I was able to take my mother quietly into the parlor, and then prepare my wife for the visit. She had drunk but little at that early hour, and luckily the devil in her was tamed for the time.

She followed me into the parlor, and the meeting passed off better than I had ventured to forecast, with this one drawback, that my mother—though she tried hard to control herself—shrank from looking my wife in the face when she spoke to her. It was a relief to me when Alicia began to prepare the table for dinner.

She laid the cloth, brought in the bread-tray, and cut some slices for us from the loaf. Then she returned to the kitchen. At that moment, while I was still anxiously watching my mother, I was startled by seeing the same ghastly change pass over her face which had altered it on the morning when Alicia and she first met. Before I could say a word, she started up with a look of horror.

"Take me back!—home, home again, Francis! Come with me, and never go back more!"

I was afraid to ask for an explanation; I could only sign to her to be silent, and help her quickly to the door. As we passed the bread-tray on the table, she stopped and pointed to it.

"Did you see what your wife cut your bread with?" she asked.

"No, mother; I was not noticing. What was it?"

"Look!".

I did look. A new clasp-knife, with a buckhorn handle, lay with the loaf in the bread-tray. I stretched out my hand to possess myself of it. At the same moment, there was a noise in the kitchen, and my mother caught me by the arm.

"The knife of the dream! Francis, I'm faint with fear—take me away before she comes back!"

I couldn't speak, to comfort or even to answer her. Superior as I was to superstition, the discovery of the knife staggered me. In silence, I helped my mother out of the house and took her home.

I held out my hand to say good-by. She tried to stop me.

"Don't go back, Francis! don't go back!"

"I must get the knife mother. I must go back by the next train."

I held to that resolution. By the next train I went back.

XII.

My wife had, of course, discovered our secret departure from the house. She had been drinking. She was in a fury of passion. The dinner in the kitchen was flung under the grate; the cloth was off the parlor table. Where was the knife?

I was foolish enough to ask for it. She refused to give it to me. In the course of the dispute between us which followed, I discovered that there was a horrible story attached to the knife. It had been used in a murder—years since—and had been so skilfully hidden that the authorities had been unable to produce it at the trial. By help of some of her disreputable friends, my wife had been enabled to purchase this relic of a bygone crime. Her perverted nature set some horrid unacknowledged value on the knife. Seeing there was no hope of getting it by fair means, I determined to search for it later in the day, in secret. The search was unsuccessful. Night came on, and I left the house to walk about the streets. You will understand what a broken man I was by this time, when I tell you I was afraid to sleep in the same room with her!

Three weeks passed. Still she refused to give up the knife; and still that fear of sleeping in the same room with her possessed me. I walked about at night or dozed in the parlor, or sat watching by my mother's bedside. Before the end of the first week in the new month, the worst misfortune of all befell me—my mother died. It wanted then but a short time of my birthday. She had longed to live till that day. I was present at her death. Her last words in this world were addressed to me:

"Don't go back, my son—don't go back!"

I was obliged to go back, if it was only to watch my wife. In the last days of my mother's illness she had spitefully added a sting to my grief by declaring that she would assert her right to attend the funeral. In spite of all that I could do or say, she held to her word. On the day appointed for the burial she forced herself—inflamed and shameless with drink—into my presence, and swore she would walk in the funeral procession to my mother's grave.

This last insult—after all I had gone through already—was more than I could endure. It maddened me. Try to make allowances for a man beside himself. I struck her.

The instant the blow was dealt, I repented it. She crouched down, silent, in a corner of the room, and eyed me steadily. It was a look that cooled my hot blood in an instant. There was no time now to think of making atonement. I could only risk the worst, and make sure of her till the funeral was over. I locked her into her bed-room.

When I came back, after laying my mother in the grave, I found her sitting by the bedside, very much altered in look and bearing, with a bundle on her lap. She faced me quietly; she spoke with a curious stillnes in her voice—strangely and unnaturally composed in look and manner.

"No man has ever struck me yet," she said. "My husband shall have no second opportunity. Set the door open and let me go."

She passed me, and left the room. I saw her walk away up the street.

Was she gone for good?

All that night I watched and waited. No footstep came near the house. The next night, overcome by fatigue, I lay down in bed in my clothes, with the door locked, the key on the table, and the candle burning. My slumber was not disturbed. The third night, the fourth, the fifth, the sixth, passed, and nothing happened. I lay down on the seventh night—still suspicious of something happening; still in my clothes; still with the door locked, the key on the table, and the candle burning. .

My rest was disturbed. I woke twice, without any sensation of uneasiness. The third time, that horrid shivering of the night at the lonely inn, that awful sinking pain at the heart, came back again and roused me in an instant.

My eyes opened toward the left-hand side of the bed. And there stood, looking at me——

The Dream-Woman again? No! My wife. The living woman, with the face of the Dream—in the attitude of the Dream—the fair arm up; the knife clasped in the delicate white hand.

I sprang upon her on the instant; but not quickly enough to stop her from hiding the knife. Without a word from me without a cry from her, I pinioned her in a chair. With one hand I felt up her sleeve; and there, where the Dream-Woman had hidden the knife, my wife had hidden it—the knife with the buckhorn handle, that looked like new.

What I felt when I made that discovery I could not realize at the time, and I can't describe now. I took one steady look at her with the knife in my hand.

"You meant to kill me?" I said.

"Yes," she answered, "I meant to kill you." She crossed her arms over her bosom, and stared me coolly in the face. "I shall do it yet," she said. "With that knife."

I don't know what possessed me—I swear to you I am no coward; and yet I acted like a coward. The horrors got hold of me. I couldn't look at her— I couldn't speak to her. I left her (with the knife in my hand), and went out into the night.

There was a bleak wind abroad, and the smell of rain was in the air. The church clocks chimed the quarter as I walked beyond the last houses in the town. I asked the first policeman I met what hour that was, of which the quarter-past had just struck. .

The man looked at his watch, and answered, "Two o'clock." Two in the morning. What day of the month was this day that had just begun ? I reckoned it up from the date of my mother's funeral. The horrid parallel between the dream and the reality was complete —it was my birthday!

Had I escaped the mortal peril which the dream foretold? or had I only received a second warning ?

As that doubt crossed my mind I stopped on my way out of the town. The air had revived me—I felt in some degree like my own self again. After a little thinking, I began to see plainly the mistake I had made in leaving my wife free to go where she liked and to do as she pleased.

I turned instantly, and made my way back to the house.

It was still dark. I had left the candle burning in the bed-chamber. When I looked up to the window of the room now, there was no light in it. I advanced to the house door. On going away I remembered to have closed it; on trying it now, I found it open.

I waited outside, never losing sight of the house till daylight. Then I ventured in-doors—listened and heard nothing—

looked into kitchen, scullery, parlor; and found nothing—went up at last into the bed-room. It was empty. A pick-lock lay on the floor, which told me how she had gained entrance in the night. And that was the one trace I could find of the Dream-Woman.

XIII.

I waited in the house till the town was astir for the day—and then I went to consult a lawyer. In the confused state of my mind at the time, I had one clear notion of what I meant to do: I was determined to sell my house and leave the neighborhood. There were obstacles in the way which I had not counted on. I was told I had creditors to satisfy before I could leave—I, who had given my wife the money to pay my bills regularly every week! Inquiry showed that she had embezzled every farthing of the money that I had entrusted to her. I had no choice but to pay over again.

Placed in this awkard position, my first duty was to set things right, with the help of my lawyer. During my forced sojourn in the town I did two foolish things. And, as a consequence that followed, I heard once more, and heard for the last time, of my wife.

In the first place, having got possession of the knife, I was rash enough to keep it in my pocket. In the second place, having something of importance to say to the lawyer, at a late hour of the evening, I went to his house after dark —alone and on foot. I got there safely enough. Returning I was seized on from behind by two men; dragged down a dark passage, and robbed—not only of the little money I had about me, but also of the knife. It was the lawyer's opinion (as it was mine) that the thieves were among the disreputable acquaint-ances formed by my wife, and that they had attacked me at her instigation. To conffim this view I received a letter the next day, with out date or address, written in Alicia's hand. The first line informed me that the knife was back again in her possession. The second line reminded me of the day when I had stuck her. The third line warned me that she would wash out the stain of that blow in my blood, and repeated the words, "I shall do it with the knife!"

These things happened, a year ago. The law laid hands on the men who had robbed me—but from that time to this the law has failed completely to find a trace of my wife.

My story is told. When I had paid the creditors and paid the legal expenses, I had barely five pounds left out of the sale of my house; and I had the world to begin over again. Some months since —driftng here and there—I found my way to Underbridge. The landlord at the inn had known something of my father's family in times past. He gave me (all he had to give) my food, and shelter in the yard. Except on market-days, there is nothing to do. In the coming winter the inn is to be shut up, and I shall have to shift for myself. My old master would help me if I applied to him—but I don't like to apply; he has done more for me already than I deserve. Besides, in another year who knows but my troubles may all be at an end? Next winter will bring me nigh to my next birthday—and my next birthday may be the day of my death. Yes! it's true I sat up all last night; and I heard two in the morning strike; and nothing happened. Still, allowing for that, time to come is a time I don't trust. My wife has got the knife—my wife is looking for me. I am above superstition, mind! I don't say I believe in dreams; I only say, Alicia Warlock is looking for me. It is possible I may be wrong. It is possible I may be right. Who can tell?

XIV.

We took leave of Francis Raven at the door of Farleigh Hall, with the understanding that he might expect to hear from us again.

The same night, Mrs. Fairbank and I had a discussion in the sanctuary of our own room. The topic was the "Ostler's Story;" and the question in dispute between us turned on the measure of charitable duty that we owed to the Ostler himself.

The view I took of the man's narrative was of the purely matter-of-fact kind. Francis Raven had, in my opinion, brooded over the misty connection between his strange dream and his vile wife, until his mind was in a state of partial delusion on that subject. I was quite willing to help him with a trifle of money, and to recommend him to the kindness of my lawyer, if he was really in any danger and wanted advice. There, my idea of my duty towards this afflicted person began and ended.

Confronted with this sensible view of the matter, Mrs. Fairbank's romantic temperament rushed as usual into extremes. "I should no more think of losing sight of Francis Raven when his next birthday comes round," says my wife, "than I should think of laying down a good story with the last chapters unread. I am positively determined, Percy, to take him back with us, when we return to France, in the capacity of groom. What does one man more or less among the horses matter to people as rich as we are?" In this strain the partner of my joys and sorrows ran on;

perfectly impenetrable to everything I could say on the side of common-sense. Need I tell my married brethren how it ended? Of course I allowed my wife to irritate me, and spoke to her sharply. Of course, my wife turned her face away indignantly on the conjugal pillow and burst into tears. Of course, upon that, "Mr." made his excuses, and "Mrs." had her own way.

Before the week was out we rode over to Underbridge, and duly offered to Francis Raven a place in our service as supernumerary groom.

At first the poor fellow seemed hardly able to realize his own extraordinary good fortune. Recovering himself, he expressed his gratitude modestly and becomingly. Mrs. Fairbank's ready sympathies overflowed as usual at her lips. She talked to him about our home in France, as if the worn, gray-headed ostler had been a child. "Such a dear old house, Francise, and such pretty gardens! Stables ten times as big as your stables here; quite a choice of roooms for you. You must learn the name of our house—it is called Maison Rouge. Our nearest town is Metz. We are within a walk of the beautiful river Moselle. And when we want a change we have only to take the railway to the frontier, and find ourselves in Germany."

Listening, so far, with a very bewildered face, Francis started and changed color, when my wife reached the end of her last sentence.

"Germany?" he repeated.

"Yes. Does Germany remind you of anything?"

The ostler's eyes looked down sadly on the ground. "Germany reminds me of my wife," he replied.

"Indeed? How?"

"She once told me she had lived in

Germany—long before I knew her—in the time when she was a young girl."

"Was she living with relations or friends?"

"She was living as governess in a foreign family."

"In what part of Germany?"

"I don't remember, ma'am. I doubt if she told me."

"Did she tell you the name of the family?"

"Yes, ma'am. It was a foreign name, and it has slipped my memory long since. The head of the family was a wine-grower in a large way of business—I remember that."

"Did you hear what sort of wine he grew? There are wine-growers in our neighborhood. Was it Moselle wine?"

"I couldn't say, ma'am. I doubt if I ever heard."

There the conversation dropped. We engaged to communicate with Francis Raven before we left England, and took our leave.

I had made my arrangements to pay our round of visits to English friends, and to return to Maison Rouge in the summer. On the eve of departure, certain difficulties in connection with the management of some landed property of mine in Ireland obliged us to alter our plans. Instead of getting back to our house in France in the summer, we only returned a week or two before Christmas. Francis Raven accompanied us, and was duly established, in the nominal capacity of stable-helper, among the servants at Maison Rouge.

Before long some of the objections to taking him into our employment, which I had foreseen and had vainly mentioned to my wife, forced themselves on our attention in no very agreeable form.

Francis Raven failed (as I had feared

he would) to get on smoothly with his fellow-servants. They were all French; and not one of them understood English.

Francis, on his side, was equally ignorant of French. His reserved manners, his melancholy temperament, his solitary ways—all told against him. Our servants called him "the English Bear." He grew widely known in the neighborhood under his nick-name. Quarrels took place, ending once or twice in blows. It became plain, even to Mrs. Fairbank herself, that some wise change must be made. While we were still considering what the change was to be, the unfortunate ostler was thrown on our hands, for some time to come, by an accident in the stables. Still pursued by his proverbial ill-luck, the poor wretch's leg was broken by a kick from a horse.

He was attended to by our own surgeon, in his comfortable bed-room at the stables. As the date of his birthday drew near he was still confined to his bed.

Physically speaking, he was doing very well. Morally speaking, the surgeon was not satisfied. Francis Raven was suffering under some unacknowledged mental disturbance, which interfered seriously with his rest at night. Hearing this, I thought it my duty to tell the medical attendant what was preying on the patient's mind. As a practical man, he shared my opinion that the ostler was in a state of delusion on the subject of his Wife and his Dream. "Curable delusion, in my opinion," the surgeon added, "if the experiment could be fairly tried."

"How can it be tried?" I asked.

Instead of replying, the surgeon put a question to me on his side.

"Do you happen to know," he said, "that this year is Leap Year?"

"Mrs. Fairbank reminded me of it;

yesterday," I answered. "Otherwise I might *not* have known it."

"Do you think Francis Raven knows that this year is Leap Year?"

(I began to see dimly what my friend was driving at.)

"It depends," I answered, "on whether he has got an English almanac. Suppose he has *not* got the almanac—what then?"

"In that case," pursued the surgeon, "Francis Raven is innocent of all suspicion that there is a twenty-ninth day in February this year. As a necessary consequence—what will he do? He will anticipate the appearance of the Woman with the Knife at 2 in the morning on the twenty-ninth day of February, instead of the first of March. Let him suffer all his superstitious terrors on the wrong day. Leave him on the day that is really his birthday, to pass a perfectly quiet night, and to be as sound asleep as other people at 2 in the morning. And then, when he wakes comfortably in time for his breakfast, shame him out of his delusion by telling him the truth."

I agree to try the experiment. Leaving the surgeon to caution Mrs. Fairbank on the subject of Leap Year, I went to the stables to see Francis Raven.

XV.

The poor fellow was full of forebodings of the fate in store for him on the ominous first of March. He eagerly entreated me to order one of the men-servants to sit up with him on the birthday morning. In granting his request, I asked him to tell me on which day of the week his birthday fell. He reckoned the days on his fingers; and proved his innocence of all suspicion that it was Leap Year by fixing on the twenty-ninth of February, in the full persuasion that it was

the first of March Pledged to try the surgeon's experiment, I left his error uncorrected, of course. In so doing, I took my first step blindfold towards the last act in the drama of the Ostler's Dream.

The next day brought with it a little domestic difficulty, which indirectly and strangely associated itself with the coming end.

My wife received a letter, inviting us to assist in celebrating the "Silver Wedding" of two worthy German neighbors of ours—Mr. and Mrs. Beldheimer. Mr. Beldheimer was a large wine-grower on the banks of the Moselle. His house was situated on the frontier line of France and Germany; and the distance from our house was sufficiently considerable to make it neccessary for us to sleep under our host's roof. Under these circumstances, if we accepted the invitation, a comparison of dates showed that we should be away from home on the morning of the first of March. Mrs. Fairbank—holding to her absurd resolution to see with her own eyes what might, or might not, happen to Francis Raven on his birthday—flatly declined to leave Maison Rouge. "It's easy to send an excuse," she said, in her off-hand manner.

I failed, for my part to see any easy way out of the difficulty. The celebration of a "Silver Wedding" in Germay is the celebration of twenty-five years of happy married life; and the host's claim upon the consideration of his friends on such an occasion is something in the nature of a Royal "command." After considerable discussion, finding my wife's obstinacy invincible, and feeling that the absence of both of us from the festival would certainly offend our friends, I left Mrs. Fairbank to make her excuses for herself; and directed her to accept the invitation as far as I was concerned. In so doing, I took my second step, blindfold, toward the last act in the drama of the Ostler's Dream.

A week elapsed; the last days of February were at hand. Another domestic difficulty happened; and, again, this event also proved to be strangely associated with the coming end.

My head groom at the stables was one Joseph Rigobert. He was an ill-conditioned fellow, inordinately vain of his personal appearance, and by no means scrupulous in his conduct with women. His one virtue consisted in his fondness for horses, and in the care he took of the animals under his charge. In a word, he was too good a groom to be easily replaced, or he would have quitted my service long since. On the occasion of which I am now writing, he was reported to me by my steward as growing idle and disorderly in his habits. The principal offence alleged against him was that he had been seen that day in the city of Metz, in the company of a woman (supposed to be an Englishwoman), whom he was entertaining at a tavern, when he ought to have been on his way back to Maison Rouge. The man's defence was that "the lady" (as he called her) was an English stranger, unacquainted with the ways of the place, and that he had only shown her where she could obtain some refreshment, at her own request. I administered the necessary reprimand—without troubling myself to inquire further into the matter. In failing to do this, I took my third step, blindfold, towards the last act in the drama of the Ostler's Dream.

On the evening of the twenty-eighth, I informed the servants at the stables that one of them must watch through the night by the Englishman's bedside. Joseph Rigobert immediately volunteered for the duty—as a means no doubt of winning his way back to my favor. I accepted his proposal.

That day, the surgeon dined with us. Towards midnight he and I left the smoking-room, and repaired to Francis Raven's bedside. Rigobert was at his post—with no very agreeable expression on his face. The Frenchman and the Englishman had evidently not got on well together, so far. Francis Raven lay helpless on his bed, waiting silently for 2 in the morning, and the Dream Woman.

"I have come, Francis, to bid you good-night," I said, cheerfully. "To-morrow morning I shall look in at breakfast time, before I leave home on a journey."

"Thank you for all your kindness, sir. You will not see me alive, tomorrow morning. She will find me, this time. Mark my words—she will find me, this time."

"My good fellow! she couldn't find you in England. How in the world is she to find you in France?"

"It's borne in on my mind, sir, that she will find me here. At 2 in the morning on my birthday I shall see her again, and see her for the last time."

"Do you mean that she will kill you?"

"I mean that, sir. She will kill me—with the knife."

"And with Rigobert in the room to protect you?"

"I am a doomed man. Fifty Rigoberts couldn't protect me."

"And yet you wanted somebody to sit up with you?"

"Mere weakness, sir. I dont like to be left alone on my death-bed."

I looked at the surgeon. If he had encouraged me, I should certainly, out of sheer compassion have confessed to Francis Raven the trick that we were playing him. The surgeon held to his experiment; the surgeon's face plainly said—"No."

The next day (the twenty-ninth of February) was the day of the Silver Wedding. The first thing in the morning, I went to Francis Raven's room. Rigobert met me at the door.

"How has he passed the night?" I asked.

"Saying his prayers, and looking for ghosts," Rigobert answered. " A lunatic asylum is the only proper place for him."

I approached the bedside. "Well, Francis, here you are, safe and sound. in spite of what you said to me, last night."

His eyes rested on mine with a vacant, wondering look.

"I don't understand it," he said.

"Did you see anything of your wife when the clock struck 2?"

"No, sir."

" Did anything happen?"

"Nothing happened, sir."

"Doesn't this satisfy you that you were wrong?"

His eyes still kept their vacant, wondering look. He only repeated the words he had spoken already:

"I don't understand it."

I made a last attempt to cheer him, "Come, come, Francis! keep a good heart. You will be out of bed in a fortnight."

He shook his head on the pillow. "There's something wrong," he said. "I don't expect you to believe me, sir. I only say, there's something wrong—and time will show it."

I left the room. Half an hour later I started for Mr. Beldheimer's house; leaving the arrangements for the morning of the first of March in the hands of the doctor and my wife.

XVI

The one thing which principally struck me when I joined the guests at the Silver Wedding is also the one thing which it is necessary to mention here. On this joyful occasion a noticeable lady present was out of spirits. That lady was no other than the heroine of the festival, the mistress of the house!

In the course of the evening, I spoke to Mr. Beldheimer's eldest son on the subject of his mother. As an old friend of the family, I had a claim on his confidence which the young man willingly recognized.

" We have had a very disagreeable matter to deal with," he said; "and my mother has not recovered the painful impression left on her mind. Many years since, when my sisters were children, we had an English governess in the house. She left us, as we then understood, to be married. We heard no more of her until a week or ten days since— when my mother received a letter in which our ex-governess described herself as being in a condition of great poverty and distress. After much hesitation she had ventured—at the suggestion of a lady who had been kind to her—to write to her former employers, and to appeal to their remembrance of old times. You know my mother; she is not only the most kindhearted, but the most innocent of women—it is impossible to persuade her of the wickedness that there is in the world. She replied by return of post, inviting the governess to come here and see her, and enclosing the money for her travelling expenses. when my father came home, and heard what had been done, he wrote at once to his agent in London to make inquiries— enclosing the address on the governess's letter. Before he could receive the agent's reply the governess arrived. She produced the worst possible impression on his mind. The agent's letter, reaching us a few days later, confirmed his suspicions. Since we had lost sight of her, the woman had led a most disreputable life. My father spoke to her privately; he offered—on condition of her leaving the house—a sum of money to take her back to England. If she refused, the alternative would be an appeal to the authorities and a public scandal. She accepted the money, and left the house. On her way back to England, she appears to have stopped at Metz. You will understand what sort of woman she is, when I tell you that she was seen, the other day, in a tavern with your handsome groom, Joseph Rigobert."

While my informant was relating these circumstances, my memory was at work. I recalled what Francis Raven had vaguely told us of his wife's experience in former days, as governess in a German family. A suspicion of the truth suddenly flashed across my mind.

"What was the woman's name?" I asked.

Mr. Beldheimer's son answered:

"Alicia Warlock."

I had but one idea when I heard that reply—to get back to my house without a moment's needless delay. It was then 10 o'clock at night—the last train to Metz had left long since. I arranged with my young friend—after duly informing him of the circumstances—that I should go by the first train in the morn-

ing, instead of staying to breakfast with the other guests who slept in the house.

At intervals during the night I wondered uneasily how things were going on at Maison Rouge. Again and again, the same question occurred to me, on my journey home in the early morning—the morning of the first of March. As the event proved, but one person in my house knew what really happened at the stables, on Francis Raven's birthday. Let Joseph Rigobert take my place as narrator, and tell the story of the end to you—as he told it, in times past, to his lawyer and to me.

———

FOURTH (AND LAST) NARRATIVE.

The Statement of Joseph Rigobert; Addressed to the Barrister who defended him at his Trial.

Respected Sir: On the twenty-seventh of February, I was sent, on business connected with the stables at Maison Rouge, to the city of Metz. On the public promenade I met a magnificent woman. Complexion blonde. Nationality, English. We mutually admired each other; we fell into conversation. (She spoke French perfectly— with the English accent.) I offered refreshment; my proposal was accepted. We had a long and interesting interview —we discovered that we were made for each other. So far, who is to blame?

Is it my fault that I am a handsome man—universally agreeable as such to the fair sex? Is it a criminal offence to be accessible to the amiable weakness of love? I ask again, who is to blame? Clearly, Nature. Not the beautiful lady —not my humble self.

To resume. The most hard-hearted person living will understand that two beings made for each other could not possibly part without an appointment to meet again.

I made arrangements for the accommodation of the lady in the village neai Maison Rouge. She consented to honor me with her company at supper, in my apartment at the stables, on the night of thet wenty-ninth. The time fixed on was the time when the other servants were accustomed to retire—11 o'clock.

Among the grooms attached to the stables was an Englishman, laid up with a broken leg. His name was Francis. His manners were repulsive; he was ignorant of the French language. In the kitchen he went by the nick-name of "The English Bear." Strange to say, he was a great favorite with my master and my mistress. They even humored certain superstitious terrors to which this repulsive person was subject—terrors into the nature of which I, as an advanced free-thinker, never thought it worth my while to inquire.

On the evening of the twenty-eighth, the Englishman, being a prey to the terrors which I have mentioned, requested that one of his fellow-servants might sit up with him for that night only. The wish that he expressed was backed by Mr. Fairbank's authority, Having already incurred my master's displeasure—in what way, a proper sense of my own dignity forbids me to relate —I volunteered to watch by the bedside of the English Bear. My object was to satisfy Mr. Fairbank that I bore no malice, on my side, after what had occurred between us. The wretched Englishman passed a night of delirium. Not understanding his barbarous language, I could only gather from his gestures that he was in deadly fear of some fancied apparition at his bedside.

From time to time, when this madman disturbed my slumbers, I quieted him by swearing at him. This is the shortest and best way of dealing with persons in his condition.

On the morning of the twenty-ninth, Mr. Fairbank left us on a journey.

Later in the day, to my unspeakable disgust, I found that I had not done with the Englishman yet. In Mr. Fairbank's absence, Mrs. Fairbank took an incomprehensible interest in the question of my delirious fellow-servant's repose at night. Again, one or other of us was to watch by his bedside, and to report it, if anything happened. Expecting my fair friend to supper, it was necessary to make sure that the other servants at the stables would be safe in their beds that night. Accordingly, I volunteered once more to be the man who kept watch. Mrs. Fairbank complimented me on my humanity. I possess great command over my feelings. I accepted the compliment without a blush.

Twice, after nightfall, my mistress and the doctor (this last staying in the house, in Mr. Fairbank's absence) came to make inquiries. Once, *before* the arrival of my fair friend—and once *after*. On the second occasion (my apartment being next door to the Englishman's) I was obliged to hide my charming guest in the harness room. She consented, with angelic resignation, to immolate her dignity to the servile necessities of my position. A more amiable woman (so far) I never met with.

After the second visit I was left free. It was then close on midnight. Up to that time, there was nothing in the behavior of the mad Englishman to reward Mrs. Fairbank and the doctor for presenting themselves at his bedside. He lay, half awake, half asleep, with an odd wondering kind of look in his face. My mistress at parting warned me to be particularly watchful of him towards 2 in the morning. The doctor (in case anything happened) left me a large hand-bell to ring, which could easily be heard at the house.

Restored to the society of my fair friend, I spread the supper-table. A pâté, a sausage, and a few bottles of generous Moselle wine, composed our simple meal. When persons adore each other, the intoxicating illusion of love transforms the simplest meal into a banquet. With immeasurable capacities for enjoyment, we sat down to table. At the very moment when I placed my fascinating companion in a chair—the infamous Englishman in the next room took that occasion of all others to become restless and noisy, once more. He struck with his stick on the floor; he cried out in a delirious access of terror, "Rigobert! Rigobert!"

The sound of that lamentable voice, suddenly assailing our ears, terrified my fair friend. She lost all her charming color in an instant. "Good heavens!" she exclaimed. "Who is that in the next room?"

"A mad Englishman."

"An Englishman?"

"Compose yourself, my angel. I will quiet him."

The lamentable voice called out on me again, "Rigobert! Rigobert!"

My fair friend caught me by the arm. "Who is he? What is his name?"

Something in her face struck me as she put that question. A spasm of jealousy shook me to the soul. "You know him?" I said.

"His name?" she vehemently repeated; "his name?"

"Francis," I answered.

"Francis—what?"

I shrugged my shoulders. I could neither remember nor pronounce the barbarous English surname. I could only tell her it began with an "R."

She dropped back into the chair. Was she going to faint? No; she recovered, and more than recovered, her lost color. Her eyes flashed superbly. What did it mean? Profoundly as I understand women in general, I was puzzled by *this* woman!

"You know him?" I repeated.

She laughed at me. "What nonsense! How should I know him? Go and quiet the wretch."

My looking-glass was near. One glance at it satisfied me that no woman in her senses could prefer the Englishman to me. I recovered my self-respect. I hastened to the Englishman's bedside.

The moment I appeared he pointed eagerly towards my room. He overwhelmed me with a torrent of words in his own language. I made out, from his gestures and his looks, that he had, in some incomprehensible manner, discovered the presence of my guest—and, stranger still, that he was scared by the idea of a person in my room. I endeavored to to compose him on the system which I have already mentioned—that is to say, I swore at him in *my* language. The result not proving satisfactory, I shook my fist in his face—and left the bed-chamber.

Returning to my fair friend, I found her walking backwards and forwards in a state of excitement wonderful to behold. She had not waited for me to fill her glass—she had begun the generous Moselle in my absence. I prevailed on her with difficulty to place herself at the table. Nothing would induce her to eat.

"My appetite is gone," she said. "Give me wine."

The generous Moselle deserves its name—delicate on the palate, with prodigious "body." The strength of this fine wine produced no stupefying effect on my remarkable guest. It appeared to strengthen and exhilarate her—nothing more. She always spoke in the same low tone, and always, turn the conversation as I might, brought it back with the same dexterity to the subject of the Englishman in the next room. In any other woman this persistency would have offended me. My lovely guest was irresistible; I answered her questions with the docility of a child. She possessed all the amusing eccentricity of her nation. When I told her of the accident which confined the Englishman to his bed, she sprang to her feet. An extraordinary smile irradiated her countenance. She said, "Show me the horse who broke his leg! 1 must, and will, see the horse!" I took her down to the stables. She kissed the horse—on my word of honor, she kissed the horse! That struck me. I said, "You do know the man; and he has wronged you in some way." No! she would not admit it, even then. "I kiss all beautiful animals," she said. "Haven't I kissed you?" With that charming explanation of her conduct, she ran back up the stairs. I only remained behind to lock the stable door again. When I rejoined her, I made a startling discovery. I cought her coming out of the Englishman s room.

"I was just going down stairs to call you," she said. "The man in there is getting noisy, once more."

The mad Englishman's voice assailed our ears again.

"Rigobert! Rigobert!"

He was a frightful object to look at when I saw him this time. His eyes were staring wildly; the perspiration was pouring over his face. In a panic of terror he clasped his hands; he pointed up to Heaven. By every sign and gesture that a man can make, he entreated me not to leave him again. I really could not help smiling. The idea of my staying with him, and leaving my fair friend by herself in the next room!

I turned to the door. When the mad wretch saw me leaving him he burst out into a screech of despair—so shrill that I feared it might awaken the sleeping servants.

My presence of mind in emergencies is proverbial among those who know me. I tore open the cupboard in which he kept his linen—seized a handful of his handkerchiefs—gagged him with one of them, and secured his hands with the others. There was now no danger of his alarming the servants. After tying the last knot, I looked up.

The door between the Englishman's room and mine was open. My fair friend was standing on the threshold—watching him as he lay helpless on the bed; watching me as I tied the last knot.

"What are you doing there?" I asked. "Why did you open the door?"

She stepped up to me, and whispered her answer in my ear—with her eyes all the time upon the man in the bed.

"I heard him scream."

"Well?"

"I thought you had killed him."

I drew back from her in horror. The suspicion of me which her words implied was sufficiently detestable in itself. But her manner when she uttered the words was more revolting still. It so powerfully affected me that I started back from that beautiful creature, as I might have recoiled from a reptile crawling over my flesh.

Before I had recovered myself sufficiently to reply, my nerves were assailed by another shock. I suddenly heard my mistress's voice, calling to me from the stable yard.

There was no time to think—there was only time to act. The one thing needful was to keep Mrs. Fairbank from ascending the stairs, and discovering—not my lady guest only—but the Englishman also, gagged and bound, on his bed. I instantly hurried to the yard. As I ran down the stairs I heard the stable clock strike the quarter to 2 in the morning.

My mistress was eager and agitated. The doctor (in attendance on her) was smiling to himself, like a man amused at his own thoughts.

"Is Francis awake or asleep?" Mrs. Fairbank inquired.

"He has been a little restless, madam. But he is now quiet again. If he is not disturbed" (I added these words to prevent her from ascending the stairs) "he will soon fall off into a quiet sleep."

"Has nothing happend since I was here last?"

"Nothing, madam."

The doctor lifted his eyebrows with a comical look of distress.

"Alas, alas, Mrs. Fairbank," he said; "nothing has happened! The days of romance are over!"

"It is not 2 o'clock yet," my mistress answered, a little irritably.

The smell of the stables was strong on the morning air. She put her handkerchief to her nose and led the way out of the yard, by the north entrance—the entrance communicating with the gardens and the house. I was ordered to follow her, along with the doctor. Once out of smell of the stables, she began to question me again. She was unwilling to believe that nothing had occurred in her absence. I invented the best answers I could think of on the spur of the moment; and the doctor stood by, laughing. So the minutes passed, till the clock struck 2. Upon that, Mrs. Fairbank announced her intention of personally visiting the Englishman in his room. To my great relief, the doctor interfered to stop her from doing this.

"You have heard that Francis is just falling asleep," he said. "If you enter his room you may disturb him. It is essential to the success of my experiment that he should have a good night's rest, and that he should own it himself, before I tell him the truth. I must request, medically, madam, that you will not disturb the man."

My mistress was unwilling to yield. For the next five minutes, at least, there was a warm discussion between the two. In the end, Mrs. Fairbank was obliged to give way—for the time. "In half an hour," she said, "Francis will either be sound asleep, or awake again. In half an hour, I shall come back." She took the doctor's arm. They returned together to the house.

Left by myself, with half an hour before me, I resolved to take the Englishwoman back to the village—then, returning to the stables, to remove the gag and the bindings from Francis, and to let him screech to his heart's content. What would his alarming the whole establishment matter to me—after I had got rid of the compromising presence of my guest?

Returning to the yard, I heard a sound like the creaking of an open door on its hinges. The gate of the north entrance I had just closed with my own hand. I went round to the west entrance at the back of the stables. It opened on a field crossed by two foot-paths, in Mr. Fairbank's grounds. The nearest footpath led to the village. The other led to the high road and the river.

Arriving at the west entrance, I found the door open—swinging to and fro in the fresh morning breeze. I had myself locked and bolted that door after admitting my fair friend at 11 o'clock. A vague dread of something wrong stole its way into my mind. I hurried back to the stables.

I looked into my own room. It was empty. I went to the harness room. Not a sign of the woman was there. I returned to my room, and approached the door of the Englishman's bedchamber. Was it possible that she had remained there during my absence? An unaccountable reluctance to open the door made me hesitate, with my hand on the lock. I listened. There was not a sound inside. I called softly. There was no answer. I drew back a step, still hesitating. I noticed something dark, moving slowly in the crevice between the bottom of the door and the boarded floor. Snatching up the candle from the table, I held it low, and looked. The dark, slowly moving object was a stream of blood!

That horrid sight roused me. I opened the door.

The Englishman lay on his bed—alone in the room. He was stabbed in two places—in the throat and in the heart. The weapon was left in the second wound. It was a knife of English manufacture, with a handle of buckhorn as good as new.

I instantly gave the alarm. Witness can speak to what followed. It is monstrous to suppose that I am guilty of the murder. I admit that I am capable of committing follies—but I shrink from the bare idea of a crime. Besides, I had no motive for killing the man. The woman murdered him, in my absence. The woman escaped by the west entrance while I was talking to my mistress. I have no more to say. I swear to you what I have here written is a true statement of all that happened on the morning of the 1st of March.

Accept, sir, the assurance of my sentiments of profound gratitude and respect.

JOSEPH RIGOBERT.

LAST LINES.
ADDED BY PERCY FAIRBANK.

Tried for the murder of Francis Raven, Joseph Rigobert was found Not Guilty; the papers of the assassinated man presenting ample evidence of the deadly animosity felt towards him by his wife.

The investigations pursued on the morning when the crime was committed showed that the murderess, after leaving the stable, had taken the footpath which led to the river. The river was dragged —without result. It remains doubtful to this day whether she died by drowning or not. The one thing certain is—that Alicia Warlock was never seen again.

So—beginning in mystery, ending in mystery—the Dream Woman passes from your view. Ghost; demon; or living human creature—say for yourselves which she is. Or, knowing what unfathomed wonders are around you, what unfathomed wonders are in you, let the wise words of the greatest of all poets be explanation enough:

" We are such stuff
As dreams are made of, and our little life
Is rounded with a sleep."

A SANE MADMAN.

ONE fine morning more than three months since, you were riding with your brother, Miss Anstell, in Hyde Park. It was a hot day; and you had allowed your horses to fall into a walking pace. As you passed the railing on the right-hand side, near the eastern extremity of the lake in the Park, neither you nor your brother noticed a solitary woman loitering on the footpath to look at the riders as they went by.

The solitary woman was my old nurse, Nancy Connell. And these were the words she heard exchanged between you and your brother, as you slowly passed her : —

Your brother said, "Is it really true that Mary Brading and her husband have gone to America?"

You laughed (as if the question amused you) and answered, "Quite true!"

"How long will they be away?" your brother asked next.

"As long as they live," you replied, with another laugh.

By this time you had passed beyond Nancy Connell's hearing. She owns to having followed your horses a few steps, to hear what was said next. She looked particularly at your brother. He 'took your reply seriously : he seemed to be quite astonished by it.

"Leave England, and settle in America!" he exclaimed. "Why should they do that?"

"Who can tell why?" you answered. "Mary Brading's husband is mad, — and Mary Brading herself is not much better."

You touched your horse with the whip, and, in a moment more, you and your brother were out of my old nurse's hearing. She wrote and told me, what I here tell you, by a recent mail. I have been thinking of those last words of yours in my leisure hours, more seriously than you would suppose. The end of it is that I take up my pen, on behalf of my husband and myself, to tell you the story of our marriage, and the reason for our emigration to the United States of America.

It matters little or nothing, to him or to me, whether our friends in England think us both mad or not. Their opinions, hostile or favorable, are of no sort of importance to us. But you are an exception to the rule. In bygone days at school we were fast and firm friends ;

and — what weighs with me even more than this — you were heartily loved and admired by my dear mother. She spoke of you tenderly on her death-bed. Events have separated us of late years. But I cannot forget the old times; and I cannot feel indifferent to your opinion of me and my husband, — though an ocean does separate us, and though we are never likely to look on one another again. It is very foolish of me, I dare say, to take seriously to heart what you said in one of your thoughtless moments. I can only plead in excuse, that I have gone through a great deal of suffering, and that I was always (as you may remember) a person of sensitive temperament, easily excited and easily depressed.

Enough of this! Do me the last favor I shall ever ask of you. Read what follows, and judge for yourself whether my husband and I are quite as mad as you were disposed to think us, when Nancy Connell heard you talking to your brother in Hyde Park.

II.

It is now more than a year since I went to Eastbourne, on the coast of Sussex, with my father and my brother James.

My brother had then, as we hoped, recovered from the effects of a fall in the hunting-field. He complained, however, at times of pain in his head; and the doctors advised us to try the sea air. We removed to Eastbourne, without a suspicion of the serious nature of the injury that he had received. For a few days all went well. We liked the place; the air agreed with us; and we determined to prolong our residence for some weeks to come.

On our sixth day at the seaside, — a memorable day to me, for reasons which you have still to learn, — my brother complained again of the old pain in his head. He and I went out together to try what exercise would do towards relieving him. We walked through the town to the fort at one end of it, and then followed a footpath running by the side of the sea, over a dreary waste of shingle, bounded at its inland extremity by the road to Hastings and by the marshy country beyond.

We had left the fort at some little distance behind us. I was walking in front, and James was following me. He was talking as quietly as usual, when he suddenly stopped in the middle of a sentence. I turned round in surprise, and discovered my brother prostrate on the path, in convulsions terrible to see.

It was the first epileptic fit I had ever witnessed. My presence of mind entirely deserted me. I could only wring my hands in horror, and scream for help. No one appeared, either from the direction of the fort or of the high road. I was too far off, I suppose, to make myself heard. Looking ahead of me, along the path, I discerned, to my infinite relief, the figure of a man running towards me. As he came nearer, I saw that he was unmistakably a gentleman, — young, and eager to be of service to me.

"Pray compose yourself!" he said, after a look at my brother. "It is very dreadful to see; but it is not dangerous. We must wait until the convulsions are over, and then I can help you."

He seemed to know so much about it that I thought he might be a medical man. I put the question to him plainly. He colored, and looked a little confused.

"I am not a doctor," he said. "I happen to have seen persons afflicted with epilepsy; and I have heard medical men say that it is useless to interfere until the fit has worn itself out. See!" he added, "your brother is quieter already. He will soon feel a sense of relief which will more than compensate him for what he has suffered. I will help him to get to the fort; and, once there, we can send for a carriage to take him home."

In five minutes more we were on our way to the fort; the stranger supporting my brother as attentively and tenderly as if he had been an old friend. When the carriage arrived he insisted on accompanying us to our own door, on the chance that his services might still be of some use. He left us, asking permission to call and inquire after James's health the next day. A more gentle and unassuming person I never met with. He not only excited my warmest gratitude — he really interested me at my first meeting with him.

I lay some stress on the impression which this young man produced upon me, — why, you will soon find out.

The next day the stranger paid his promised visit of inquiry. His card, which he sent upstairs, informed us that his name was Roland Cameron. My father — who is not easily pleased — took a liking to him at once. His visit was prolonged, at our request. In the course of conversation, he said just enough about himself to satisfy us that we were receiving a person who was at least of equal rank with ourselves. Born in England, of a Scotch family, he had lost both his parents. Not long since he had inherited a fortune from one of his uncles. It struck us as a little strange that he spoke of this fortune with a marked change to melancholy in his voice and in his manner. The subject was, for some inconceivable reason, evidently distasteful to him. Rich as he was, he acknowledged that he led a simple and solitary life. He had little taste for society, and no sympathies in common with the average young men of his own age. But he had his own harmless pleasures and occupations; and past sorrow and suffering had taught him not to expect too much from life. All this was said modestly, with a winning charm of look and voice which indescribably attracted me. His personal appearance aided the favorable impression which his manner and his conversation produced. He was of the middle height, lightly and firmly built; his complexion pale; his hands and feet small and finely shaped; his brown hair curling naturally; his eyes large and dark, with an occasional indecision in their expression which was far from being an objection to them, to my taste. It seemed to harmonize with an occasional indecision in his talk; proceeding, as I was inclined to think, from some passing confusion in his thoughts which it always cost him a little effort to discipline and overcome. Does it surprise you to find how closely I observed a man who was only a chance acquaintance, at my first interview with him? Or do your suspicious enlighten you, and do you say to yourself, She has fallen in love with Mr. Roland Cameron at first sight? I may plead, in my own defence, that I was not quite romantic enough to go that length. But I own I waited for his next visit with an impatience which was new to me in my experience of my sober self. And worse still, when the day came, I changed my dress three times, before my newly developed vanity was satisfied with the picture which the looking-glass presented to me of myself!

In a fortnight more my father and my brother began to look on the daily companionship of our new friend as one of the settled institutions of their lives. In a fortnight more Mr. Roland Cameron and I — though we neither of us ventured to acknowledge it — were as devotedly in love with each other as two young people could well be. Ah, what a delightful time it was! and how cruelly soon our happiness came to an end!

During the brief interval which I have just described I observed certain peculiarities in Roland Cameron's conduct which perplexed and troubled me, when my mind was busy with him in my lonely moments.

For instance, he was subject to the strangest lapses into silence when he and I were talking together. They seized him suddenly, in the most capricious manner; sometimes when he was speaking, sometimes when I was speaking. At these times, his eyes assumed a weary, absent look, and his mind seemed to wander away, — far from the conversation and far from me. He was perfectly unaware of his own infirmity: he fell into it unconsciously, and came out of it unconsciously. If I noticed that he had not been attending to me, or if I asked why he had been silent, he was completely at a loss to comprehend what I meant. What he was thinking of in these pauses of silence it was impossible to guess. His face, at other times singularly mobile and expressive, became almost a perfect blank. Had he suffered some terrible shock, at some past period of his life? and had his mind never quite recovered it? I longed to ask him the question, and yet I shrank from doing it, — I was so sadly afraid of distressing him; or, to put it in plainer words, I was so truly and so tenderly fond of him.

Then, again, though he was ordinarily the most gentle and most lovable of men, there were occasions when he would surprise me by violent outbreaks of temper, excited by the merest trifles. A dog barking suddenly at his heels, or a boy throwing stones in the road, or an importunate shop-keeper trying to make him purchase something that he did not want, would throw him into a frenzy of rage which was, without exaggeration, really alarming to see. He always apologized for these outbreaks, in terms which showed that he was sincerely ashamed of his own violence. But he could never succeed in controlling himself. The lapses into passion, like the lapses into silence, took him into their own possession, and did with him, for the time being, just what they pleased.

One more example of Roland's peculiarities, and I have done. The strangeness of his conduct, in this case, was noticed by my father and my brother as well as by me.

When Roland was with us in the evening, whether he came to dinner or to tea, he invariably left us exactly at nine o'clock. Try as we might to persuade him to stay longer, he always politely but positively refused. Even I had no influence over him in this matter. When I pressed him to remain, — though it cost him an effort, — he still persisted in retiring exactly as the clock struck nine. He gave no reason for this strange proceeding; he only said that it was a habit of his, and begged us to indulge him, without asking for any further explanation. My father and my brother (being men) succeeded in controlling their curiosity. For my part (being a woman), every day that passed only made me more and more eager to penetrate the mystery. I privately resolved to choose my time, when Roland was in a particularly accessible humor, and then to appeal to him for the explanation which he had hitherto refused, as a special favor granted to myself.

In two days more I found my opportunity.

Some friends of ours, who had joined us at Eastbourne, proposed a picnic party to the famous neighboring cliff called Beachy Head. We accepted the invitation. The day was lovely, and the gypsy dinner was, as usual, infinitely preferable (for once in a way) to a formal dinner in-doors. Towards the evening our little assembly separated into parties of two and three, to explore the neighborhood. Roland and I found ourselves together, as a matter of course. We were happy, and we were alone.

Was it the right or the wrong time to ask the fatal question? I am not able to decide, — I only know that I asked it.

III.

"Mr. Cameron," I said, "will you make allowances for a weak woman? And will you tell me something that I am dying to know?"

He walked straight into the trap, — with that entire absence of ready wit, or small suspicion (I leave you to choose the right phrase), which is so like men, and so little like women.

"Of course I will!" he answered.

"Then, tell me," I asked, "why do you always insist on leaving us at nine o'clock?"

He started, and looked at me, so sadly, so reproachfully, that I would have given everything I possessed to recall the rash words that had just passed my lips.

"If I consent to tell you," he replied, after a momentary struggle with himself, "will you let me put a question to you first? and will you promise to answer it?"

I gave him my promise, and waited eagerly for what was coming next.

"Miss Brading," he said, "tell me honestly, do you think I am mad?"

It was impossible to laugh at him; he spoke those strange words seriously, sternly I might almost say.

"No such thought ever entered my mind," I answered.

He looked at me very earnestly.

"You say that, on your word of honor?"

"On my word of honor."

I answered with perfect sincerity; and I evidently satisfied him that I had spoken the truth. He took my hand, and lifted it gratefully to his lips.

"Thank you," he said simply. "You encourage me to tell you a very sad story."

"Your own story!" I asked.

"My own story. Let me begin by telling you why I persist in leaving your house always at the same early hour. Whenever I go out, I am bound by a promise to the person with whom I am living here, to return at a quarter past nine o'clock."

"The person with whom you are living?" I repeated. "You are living at a boarding-house, are you not?"

"I am living, Miss Brading, under the care of a doctor who keeps an asylum for the insane. He has taken a house for some of his wealthier patients at the seaside; and he allows me my liberty in the daytime, on the condition that I faithfully perform my promise at night. It is a quarter of an hour's walk from your house to the doctor's; and it is a rule that the patients retire at half-past nine o'clock."

Here was the mystery, which had so sorely perplexed me, revealed at last! The disclosure literally struck me speechless. Unconsciously and instinctively I drew back from him a few steps. He fixed his sad eyes on me with a touching look of entreaty.

"Don't shrink away from me!" he said. "You don't think I am mad?"

I was too confused and distressed to know what to say; and, at the same time, I was too fond of him not to answer that appeal. I took his hand and pressed it in silence. He turned his head aside for a moment. I thought I saw a tear on his cheek; I felt his hand close tremblingly on mine. He mastered himself with surprising resolution; he spoke with perfect composure when he looked at me again.

"Do you care to hear my story," he asked, "after what I have just told you?"

"I am eager to hear it," I answered.

"You do not know how I feel for you! I am too distressed to be able to express myself in words."

"You are the kindest and dearest of women!" he said, with the utmost fervor and at the same time with the utmost respect.

We sat down together in a grassy hollow of the cliff, with our faces towards the grand gray sea. The daylight was beginning to fade, as I heard the story which made me Roland Cameron's wife.

IV.

"My mother died when I was an infant in arms," he began. "My father, from my earliest to my latest recollections, was always hard towards me. I have been told that I was an odd child, with strange ways of my own. My father detested anything that was strongly marked, anything out of the ordinary way, in the characters and habits of the persons about him. He himself lived (as the phrase is) by line and rule; and he determined to make his son follow his example. I was subjected to severe discipline at school, and I was carefully watched afterwards at college. Looking back on my early life, I can see no traces of happiness, I can find no tokens of sympathy. Sad submission to a hard destiny, weary wayfaring over unfriendly roads, — such is the story of my life, from ten years old to twenty.

"I passed one autumn vacation at the Lakes; and there I met by accident with a young French lady. The result of that meeting decided my whole after-life.

"She filled the humble position of nursery-governess in the house of a wealthy Englishman. I had frequent opportunities of seeing her. Her life had been a hard one, like mine. We took an innocent pleasure in each other's society. Her little experience of life was strangely like mine: there was a perfect sympathy of thought and feeling between us. We loved, or thought we loved. I was not twenty-one, and she was not eighteen, when I asked her to be my wife.

"I can understand my folly now, and can laugh at it or lament over it, as the humor moves me. And yet, I can't help pitying myself, when I look back at myself at that time, — I was so young, so hungry for a little sympathy, so weary of my empty, friendless life! Well, everything is comparative in this world. I was soon to regret, bitterly to regret, that friendless life, wretched as it was.

"The poor girl's employer found out our attachment, through his wife. He at once communicated to my father.

"My father had but one word to say, — he insisted on my going abroad, and leaving it to him to release me from my absurd engagement, in my absence.

I answered him that I should be of age in a few months, and that I was determined to marry the girl. He gave me three days to reconsider my resolution. I held to my resolution. In a week afterwards, I was declared insane by two medical men, and I was placed by my father in a lunatic asylum.

"Was it an act of insanity for the son of a gentleman, with great expectations before him, to propose marriage to a nursery-governess? I declare, as God is my witness, I know of no other act of mine which could justify my father, and justify the doctors, in placing me under restraint.

"I was three years in the asylum. It was officially reported that the air did not agree with me. I was removed, for two years more, to another asylum, in a remote part of England. For the five best years of my life I have been herded with madmen, — and my reason has survived it. The impression I produce on you, on your father, on your brother, on all our friends at this picnic, is that I am as reasonable as the rest of my fellow-creatures. Am I rushing to a hasty conclusion, when I assert myself to be now, and always to have been, a sane man?

"At the end of my five years of arbitrary imprisonment in a free country, happily for me, — I am ashamed to say it, but I must speak the truth, — happily for me, my merciless father died. His trustees, to whom I was now consigned, felt some pity for me. They could not take the responsibility of granting me my freedom. But they placed me under the care of a surgeon, who received me into his private residence, and who allowed me free exercise in the open air.

"A year's trial in this new mode of life satisfied the surgeon, and satisfied every one else who took the smallest interest in me, that I was perfectly fit to enjoy my liberty. I was freed from all restraint, and was permitted to reside with a near relative of mine, in that very Lake country which had been the scene of my fatal meeting with the French girl, six years since.

"In this retirement I lived happily, satisfied with the ordinary pleasures and pursuits of a country gentleman. Time had long since cured me of my boyish infatuation for the nursery-governess. I could revisit with perfect composure the paths along which we had walked, the lake on which we had sailed together. Hearing by chance that she was married in her own country, I could wish her all possible happiness, with the sober kindness of a disinterested friend. What a strange thread of irony runs through the texture of the simplest human life! The early love, for which I had sacrificed and suffered so much, was now revealed to me, in its true colors, as a boy's passing fancy, — nothing more!

"Three years of peaceful freedom passed; freedom which, on the uncontradicted testimony of respectable witnesses, I never abused. Well, that long and happy interval, like all intervals, came to its end; and then the great misfortune of my life fell upon me. One of my uncles died and left me inheritor of his whole fortune. I alone, to the exclusion of all the other heirs, now received, not only the large income derived from his estates, but seventy thousand pounds in ready money as well.

"The vile calumny which had asserted me to be mad was now revived by the wretches interested in stepping between me and my inheritance. A year ago, I was sent back again to the asylum in which I had been last imprisoned. The pretence for confining me was found in an act of violence (as it was called) which I had committed in a momentary outbreak of anger, and which it was acknowledged had led to no serious results. Having got me into the asylum, the conspirators proceeded to complete their work. A commission in Lunacy was issued against me. It was held by one commissioner, without a jury, and without the presence of a lawyer to assert my interests. By one man's decision, I was declared to be of unsound mind. The custody of my person, and the management of my estates, was confided to men chosen from among the conspirators who had declared me to be mad. I am here through the favor of the proprietor of the asylum, who has given me my holiday at the seaside, and who humanely trusts me with my liberty, as you see. At barely thirty years old I am refused the free use of my money and the free management of my affairs. At barely thirty years old I am officially declared to be a lunatic for life."

V.

HE paused; his head sank on his breast; his story was told.

I have repeated his words as nearly as I can remember them; but I can

"I DON'T KNOW HOW IT HAPPENED. I FOUND MYSELF IN HIS ARMS, AND
I ANSWERED HIM WITH A KISS." — Page 51.

give no idea of the modest and touching resignation with which he spoke. To say that I pitied him with my whole heart, is to say nothing. I loved him with my whole heart, — and I may acknowledge it now!

"O Mr. Cameron," I said, as soon as I could trust myself to speak, "can nothing be done to help you? Is there no hope?"

"There is always hope," he answered, without raising his head. "I have to thank *you*, Miss Brading, for teaching me that."

"To thank me?" I repeated. "How have I taught you to hope?"

"You have brightened my dreary life. When I am with you, all my bitter remembrances leave me. I am a happy man again; and a happy man can always hope. I dream now of finding, what I have never yet had, a dear and devoted friend, who will rouse the energy that has sunk in me under the martyrdom that I have endured. Why do I submit to the loss of my rights and my liberty, without an effort to recover them? I was alone in the world, until I met with you. I had no kind hand to raise me, no kind voice to encourage me. Shall I ever find the hand? Shall I ever hear the voice? When I am with you, the hope that you have taught me answers, Yes. When I am by myself, the old despair comes back, and answers, No."

He lifted his head for the first time. If I had not understood what his words meant, his look would have enlightened me. The tears came into my eyes; my heart heaved and fluttered wildly; my hands mechanically tore up and scattered the grass around me. The silence became unendurable. I spoke, hardly knowing what I was saying; tearing faster and faster the poor harmless grass, as if my whole business in life was to pull up the greatest quantity in the shortest possible space of time.

"We have only known each other a little while," I said. "And a woman is but a weak ally in such a terrible position as yours. But useless as I may be, count on me now and always as your friend — "

He moved close to me before I could say more, and took my hand. He murmured in my ear, —

"May I count on you, one day, as the nearest and dearest friend of all? Will you forgive me, Mary, if I own that I love you? You have taught me to love, as you have taught me to hope. It is in your power to lighten my hard lot. *You* can recompense me for all that I have suffered; *you* can rouse me to struggle for my freedom and my rights. Be the good angel of my life. Forgive me, love me, rescue me, — be my wife!"

I don't know how it happened. I found myself in his arms, and I answered him in a kiss. Taking all the circumstances into consideration, I daresay I was guilty, in accepting him, of the rashest act that ever a woman committed. Very well. I didn't care then; I don't care now. I was then, and I am now, the happiest woman living!

VI.

It was necessary that either he or I should tell my father of what had passed between us. On reflection, I thought

it best that I should make the disclosure. The day after the picnic I repeated to my father Roland's melancholy narrative, as a necessary preface
to the announcement that I had promised
to be Roland's wife.

My father saw the obvious objections
to the marriage. He warned me of the
imprudence which I contemplated committing, in the strongest terms. Our
prospect of happiness, if we married, in
our present position, would depend
entirely on our capacity to legally
supersede the proceedings of the Lunacy
Commission. Success in this arduous
undertaking was, to say the least of it,
uncertain. The commonest prudence
pointed to the propriety of delaying our
marriage until the doubtful experiment
had been put to the proof.

This reason was unanswerable. It
was, nevertheless, completely thrown
away upon me. When did a woman in
love ever listen to reason? I believe
there is no instance of it on record.
My father's wise words of caution had
no chance against Roland's fervent entreaties. The days of his residence at
Eastbourne were drawing to a close.
If I let him return to the asylum an
unmarried man, months, years perhaps,
might pass before our union could take
place. Could I expect him, could I
expect any man, to endure that cruel
separation, that unrelieved suspense?
His mind had been sorely tried already;
his mind might give way under it.
These were the arguments that carried
weight with them, in my judgment. I
was of age, and free to act as I pleased.
You are welcome, if you like, to consider
me the most foolish and the most obsti-

nate of women. In sixteen days from
the date of the picnic, Roland and I
were privately married at Eastbourne.

My father — more grieved than angry,
poor man ! — declined to be present at
the ceremony, in justice to himself.
My brother gave me away at the altar.

Roland and I spent the afternoon of
the wedding-day and the earlier part of
the evening together. At nine o'clock,
he returned to the doctor's house, exactly as usual ; having previously explained
to me that he was in the power of the
Court of Chancery, and that until we
succeeded in setting aside the proceedings of the Lunacy Commission, there
was a serious necessity for keeping the
marriage strictly secret. My husband
and I kissed, and said good-by till tomorrow, as the clock struck the hour.
I little thought, while I looked after him
from the street door, that months on
months were to pass before I saw
Roland again.

A hurried note from my husband
reached me the next morning. Our
marriage had been discovered (we
never could tell by whom), and we had
been betrayed to the doctor. Roland
was then on his way back to the asylum. He had been warned that force
would be used if he resisted. Knowing that resistance would be interpreted,
in his case, as a new outbreak of madness, he had wisely submitted. "I
have made the sacrifice," the letter concluded, "It is now for you to help me.
Attack the Commission in Lunacy, and
be quick about it."

We lost no time in preparing for the
attack. On the day when I received
the news of our misfortune, we left

Eastbourne for London, and at once took measures to obtain the best legal advice.

My dear father — though I was far from deserving his kindness — entered into the matter heart and soul. In due course of time we presented a petition to the Lord Chancellor, praying that the decision of the Lunacy Commission might be set aside.

We supported our petition by citing the evidence of Roland's friends and neighbors, during his three years' residence in the Lake country as a free man. These worthy people had one and all agreed that he was, as to their judgment and experience, perfectly quiet, harmless and sane. Many of them had gone out shooting with him. Others had often accompanied him in sailing excursions on the lake. Do people trust a madman with a gun, and with the management of a boat? As to the "act of violence," which the heirs at law and the next of kin had made the means of imprisoning Roland in the mad-house, it had amounted to this. He had lost his temper, and had knocked a man down who had offended him. Very wrong, no doubt; but if *that* is a proof of madness, what thousands of lunatics are still at large! Another instance produced to prove his insanity was still more absurd. It was solemnly declared that he put an image of the Virgin Mary in his boat when he went out on his sailing excursions! I have seen the image, — it was a very beautiful work of art. Was Roland mad to admire it, and take it with him? His religious convictions leaned towards Catholicism. If he betrayed insanity in adorning his boat with an image of the Virgin Mary, what is the mental condition of most of the ladies in Christendom, who wear the Cross as an ornament round their necks? We advanced these arguments in our petition, after quoting the evidence of the witnesses. And, more than this, we even went the length of admitting, as an act of respect to the Court, that my poor husband might be eccentric in some of his opinions and habits. But we put it to the authorities whether better results might not be expected from placing him under the care of a wife who loved him, and whom he loved, than from shutting him up in an asylum, among incurable madmen as his companions for life.

Such was our petition, so far as I am able to describe it.

The decision rested with the Lords Justices. They decided against us.

Turning a deaf ear to our witnesses and our arguments, these merciless lawyers declared that the doctor's individual assertion of my husband's insanity was enough for them. They considered Roland's comfort to be sufficiently provided for in the asylum, with an allowance of seven hundred pounds a year; and to the asylum they consigned him for the rest of his days.

So far as I was concerned, the result of this infamous judgment was to deprive me of the position of Roland's wife; no lunatic being capable of contracting marriage by law. So far as my husband was concerned, the result may be best stated in the language of a popular newspaper which published an article on the case. "It is possible," (said the article, — I' wish I could personally thank the man who wrote it!) "for the Court of Chancery to take a man who has a large fortune, and is in the prime of life, but is a little touched in the head, and make a monk of him, and then report to itself that the comfort and happiness of the lunatic have been effectually provided for at the expenditure of seven hundred pounds a year."

Roland was determined, however, that they should *not* make a monk of him; and, you may rely upon it, so was I!

But one alternative was left to us. The authority of the Court of Chancery (within its jurisdiction) is the most despotic authority on the face of the earth. Our one hope was in taking to flight. The price of our liberty, as citizens of England, was exile from our native country, and the entire abandonment of Roland's fortune. We accepted those hard conditions. Hospitable America offered us a refuge, beyond the reach of mad-doctors and Lords Justices. To hospitable America our hearts turned as to our second country. The serious question was, — how were we to get there?

We had attempted to correspond, and had failed. Our letters had been discovered and seized by the proprietor of the asylum. Fortunately, we had taken the precaution of writing in a "cipher" of Roland's invention, which he had taught me before our marriage. Though our letters were illegible, our purpose was suspected, as a matter of course; and a watch was kept on my husband, night and day.

Foiled in our first effort at making arrangements secretly for our flight, we continued our correspondence (still in cipher), by means of advertisements in the newspapers. This second attempt was discovered in its turn. Roland was refused permission to subscribe to the newspapers, and was forbidden to enter the reading-room at the asylum.

These tyrannical prohibitions came too late. Our plans had already been communicated: we understood each other, and we had now only to bide our time. We had arranged that my brother, and a friend of his, on whose discretion we could thoroughly rely, should take it in turns to watch every evening, for a given time, at an appointed meeting-place, three miles distant from the asylum. The spot had been carefully chosen. It was on the bank of a lonely stream, and close to the outskirts of a thick wood. A water-proof knapsack, containing a change of clothes, a false beard and a wig, and some biscuits and preserved meat, was hidden in a hollow tree. My brother and his friend always took their fishing-rods with them, and presented themselves as engaged in the innocent occupation of angling, to any chance strangers who might pass within sight of them. On one occasion the proprietor of the asylum himself rode by them, on the opposite bank of the stream, and asked politely if they had had good sport!

For a fortnight these stanch allies of ours relieved each other regularly on their watch, and no signs of the fugitive appeared. On the fifteenth evening, just as the twilight was changing into night, and just as my brother (whose turn it was) had decided on leaving the place, Roland suddenly joined him on the bank of the stream.

Without wasting a moment in words, the two at once entered the wood, and took the knapsack from its place of shelter in the hollow tree. In ten minutes more, my husband was dressed in a suit of workman's clothes, and was further disguised in the wig and beard. The two then set forth down the course of the stream, keeping in the shadow of the wood until the night had fallen and the darkness hid them. The night was cloudy; there was no moon. After walking two miles, or a little more, they altered their course, and made boldly for the high road to Manchester; entering on it at a point some thirty miles distant from the city.

On their way from the wood, Roland described the manner in which he had effected his escape.

The story was simple enough. He had assumed to be suffering from nervous illness, and had requested to have his meals in his own room. For the first fortnight, the two men appointed to wait upon him in succession, week by week, were both more than his match in strength. The third man employed, at the beginning of the third week, was, physically, a less formidable person than his predecessors. Seeing this, Roland decided, when evening came, on committing another "act of violence." In plain words, he sprang upon the keeper, waiting on him in his room, and gagged and bound the man. This done, he laid the unlucky keeper (face to the wall) on his own bed, covered with his own cloak, so that any one entering the room might suppose that he was lying down to rest. He had previously taken the precaution to remove the sheets from the bed; and he had now only to tie them together to escape by the window of his room, situated on the upper floor of the house. The sun was setting, and the inmates of the asylum were at tea. After narrowly missing discovery by one of the laborers employed in the grounds, he had climbed the garden enclosure, and had dropped on the other side, a free man!

Arrived on the high road to Manchester, my husband and my brother parted.

Roland, who was an excellent walker, set forth on his way to Manchester on foot. He had food in his knapsack, and he proposed to walk some twelve or fifteen miles on the road to the city, before he stopped at any town or village to rest. My brother, who was physically incapable of accompanying him, returned to the place in which I was then residing, to tell me the good news.

By the first train the next morning I travelled to Manchester, and took a lodging in a suburb of the city well known to my husband. A prim, smoky little square was in the immediate neighborhood; and we had arranged that whichever of us first arrived in Manchester should walk round that square, between twelve and one in the afternoon, and between six and seven in the evening. In the evening I kept my appointment. A dusty, footsore man, in shabby clothes, with a hideous beard, and a knapsack on his back, met me at my first walk round. He smiled as I looked at him. Ah! I knew that smile through all disguises! In spite of the Court of Chancery and the Lords Justices, I was in my husband's arms once more.

We lived quietly in our retreat for a month.

During that time (as I heard by letters from my brother) nothing that money and cunning could do, towards discovering Roland, was left untried by the proprietor of the asylum and by the persons acting with him. But where is the cunning which can trace a man, who, escaping at night in disguise, has not trusted himself to a railway or a carriage, and who takes refuge in a great city in which he has no friends? At the end of one month in Manchester, we travelled northward; crossed the channel to Ireland, and passed a pleasant fortnight in Dublin. Leaving this again, we made our way to Cork and Queenstown, and embarked from that latter place, taking steerage passage in a steamship bound for America.

My story is told. I am writing these lines from a farm in the west of the United States. Our neighbors may be homely enough, but the roughest of them is kinder to us than a mad-doctor or a Lord Justice. Roland is happy in those agricultural pursuits which have always been favorite pursuits with him; and I am happy with Roland. Our sole resources consist of my humble little fortune, inherited from my dear mother. After deducting our travelling expenses, the sum total amounts to between seven and eight hundred pounds; and this, as we find, is amply sufficient to start us in the new life that we have chosen. We expect my father and my brother to pay us a visit next summer; and I think it just possible that they may find our family circle increased by the presence of a new member in long clothes. Are there no compensations here, for exile from England and the loss of a fortune? We think there are. But then, my dear Miss Anstell, "Mary Brading's husband is mad; and Mary Brading herself is not much better."

If you feel inclined to alter this opinion, and if you remember our old days at school as tenderly as I remember them, write and tell me so. Your letter will be forwarded, if you send it to the enclosed address at New York.

In the mean time, the moral of our story seems to be worthy of serious consideration. A certain Englishman legally inherits a large fortune. At the time of his inheritance he has been living as a free man for three years, without once abusing his freedom, and with the express sanction of the medical superintendent who has had experience and charge of him. His next of kin and heirs at law (who are left out of the fortune) look with covetous eyes at the money, and determine to get the management and the ultimate possession of it. Assisted by a doctor, whose honesty and capacity must be taken on trust, these interested persons, in this nineteenth century of progress, can lawfully imprison their relative for life, in a country which calls itself free, and which declares that its justice is equally administered to all alike.

NOTE. — The reader is informed that this story is founded, in all essential particulars, on a case which actually occurred in England, eight years since.

W. C.

THE FATAL CRADLE:

OTHERWISE,

THE HEART-RENDING STORY OF MR. HEAVYSIDES.

THERE has never yet been discovered a man with a grievance, who objected to mention it. I am no exception to this general human rule. I have got a grievance, and I don't object to mention it. Compose your spirits to hear a pathetic story, and kindly picture me in your own mind as a baby five minutes old.

Do I understand you to say that I am too big and too heavy to be pictured in anybody's mind as a baby? Perhaps I may be — but don't mention my weight again, if you please. My weight has been the grand misfortune of my life. It spoiled all my prospects (as you will presently hear) before I was two days old.

My story begins thirty-one years ago, at eleven o'clock in the forenoon, and starts with the great mistake of my first appearance in this world, at sea, on board the merchant ship *Adventure*, Captain Gillop, five hundred tons burden, coppered, and carrying an experienced surgeon.

In presenting myself to you (which I am now about to do) at that eventful period of my life when I was from five to ten minutes old, and in withdrawing myself again from your notice (so as not to trouble you with more than a short story) before the time when I cut my first tooth, I need not hesitate to admit that I speak on hearsay knowledge only. It is knowledge, however, that may be relied on, for all that. My information comes from Captain Gillop, commander of the *Adventure* (who sent it to me in the form of a letter) ; from Mr. Jolly, experienced surgeon of the *Adventure* (who wrote it for me — most unfeelingly, as I think — in the shape of a humorous narrative) ; and from Mrs. Drabble, stewardess of the *Adventure* (who told it me by word of mouth). Those three persons were, in various degrees, spectators — I may say astonished spectators — of the events which I have now to relate.

The *Adventure*, at the time I speak of, was bound out from London to Australia. I suppose you know without my telling you that thirty years ago was long before the time of the gold-finding and the famous clipper ships. Building in the new colony and sheep-farming far up inland were the two main employments of those days, and the passengers on board our vessel were consequently builders or sheep-farmers, almost to a man.

A ship of five hundred tons, well loaded with cargo, doesn't offer first-rate accommodations to a large number of passengers. Not that the gentlefolks in the cabin had any great reason to complain. There the passage-money, which was a good, round sum, kept them what you call select. One or two berths in this part of the ship were even empty and going a-begging, in consequence of there being only four cabin passengers. These are their names and descriptions : —

Mr. Sims, a middle-aged man, going out on a building speculation ; Mr. Purling, a weakly young gentleman, sent on a long sea-voyage, for the benefit of his health ; and Mr. and Mrs. Smallchild, a young married couple, with a little independence, which Mr. Smallchild proposed to make a large one by sheep-farming.

This gentleman was reported to the captain as being very good company when on shore. But the sea altered him to a certain extent. When Mr. Smallchild was not sick, he was eating and drinking ; and when he was not eating and drinking, he was fast asleep. He was perfectly patient and good-humored, and wonderfully nimble at running into his cabin when the qualms took him on a sudden ; but, as for his being good company, nobody heard him say ten words together all through the voyage. And no wonder. A man can't talk in the qualms ; a man can't talk while he is eating and drinking ; and a man can't talk when he is asleep. And that was Mr. Smallchild's life.

As for Mrs. Smallchild, she kept her cabin from first to last. But you will hear more of her presently.

These four cabin passengers, as I have already remarked, were well enough off for their accommodation. But the miserable people in the steerage — a poor place at the best of times on board the *Adventure* — were all huddled together, men and women and children, higgledy-piggledy, like sheep in a pen, except that they hadn't got the same quantity of fine fresh air to blow over them. They were artisans and farm-laborers, who couldn't make it out in the Old Country. I have no information either of their exact numbers or of their names. It doesn't matter ; there was only one family among them which need be mentioned particularly — namely, the family of the Heavysides. To wit, Simon Heavysides, intelligent and well-educated, a carpenter by trade ; Susan Heavysides, his wife ; and seven little Heavysides, their unfortunate offspring. My father and mother and brothers and sisters, did I understand you to say ? Don't be in a hurry ! I recommend you to wait a little before you make quite sure of that circumstance.

Though I myself had not, perhaps, strictly speaking, come on board when the vessel left London, my ill luck, as I firmly believe, had shipped in the *Adventure* to wait for me — and decided the nature of the voyage accordingly.

Never was such a miserable time known. Stormy weather came down on us from all points of the compass, with intervals of light, baffling winds or dead calms. By the time the *Adventure* had been three months out, Captain Gillop's naturally sweet temper began to get soured. I leave you to say whether it was likely to be much improved by a piece of news which reached him from the region of the cabin on the morning of the ninety-first day. It had fallen to a dead calm again : and the ship was rolling about helpless, with her head all round the compass, when Mr. Jolly (from whose facetious narrative I repeat all conversations exactly as they passed) came on deck to the captain, and addressed him in these words : —

" I have got some news that will rather surprise you," said Mr. Jolly, smiling and rubbing his hands. (Although the experienced surgeon has not shown much sympathy for my troubles, I won't deny that his disposition was as good as his name. To this day no amount of bad weather or hard work can upset Mr. Jolly's temper.)

" If it's news of a fair wind coming," grumbled the captain, " that would surprise me on board this ship, I can promise you ! "

" It's not exactly a wind coming," said Mr. Jolly. " It's another cabin passenger."

The captain looked round at the empty sea, with the land thousands of miles away, and with not a ship in sight — turned sharply on the experienced surgeon — eyed him hard — changed color suddenly — and asked what he meant.

" I mean there's a fifth cabin passenger coming on board," persisted Mr. Jolly, grinning from ear to ear, — " introduced by Mrs. Smallchild — likely to join us, I should say, toward evening — size, nothing to speak of — sex, not known at present — manners and customs, probably squally."

" Do you really mean it ? " asked the captain, backing away, and turning paler and paler.

" Yes, I do," answered Mr. Jolly, nodding hard at him.

" Then I'll tell you what," cried Captain Gillop, suddenly flying into a violent passion, " I won't have it ! the infernal weather has worried me out of my life and soul already — and I won't have it ! Put it off, Jolly, — tell her there isn't room enough for that sort of thing on board my vessel. What does she mean by taking us all in in this way ? Shameful ! Shameful ! "

" No ! no ! " remonstrated Mr. Jolly. " Don't look at it in that light. It's her first child, poor thing. How should *she* know ? Give her a little more experience, and I dare say — "

" Where's her husband ? " broke in the captain, with a threatening look. " I'll speak my mind to her husband, at any rate."

Mr. Jolly consulted his watch before he answered.

" Half-past eleven," he said. " Let me consider a little. It's Mr. Smallchild's regular time just now for squaring accounts with the sea. He'll have done in a quarter of an hour. In five minutes more he'll be fast asleep. At one o'clock he'll eat a hearty lunch, and go to sleep again. At half-past two he'll square accounts as before — and so on till night. You'll make nothing out of Mr. Smallchild, captain. Extraordinary man — wastes tissue, and repairs it again perpetually, in the most astonishing manner. If we are another month at sea, I believe we shall bring him into port totally comatose. — Halloo! What do *you* want?"

The steward's mate had approached the quarter-deck while the doctor was speaking. Was it a curious coincidence? This man also was grinning from ear to ear, exactly like Mr. Jolly.

"You're wanted in the steerage, sir," said the steward's mate to the doctor. "A woman taken bad, name of Heavysides."

"Nonsense!" cried Mr. Jolly. "Ha, ha, ha! You don't mean — eh?"

"That's it, sir, sure enough," said the steward's mate, in the most positive manner.

Captain Gillop looked all around him in silent desperation; lost his sea-legs for .the first time these twenty years; staggered back till he was brought all standing by the side of his own vessel; dashed his fist on the bulwark, and found language to express himself in, at the same moment.

"This ship is bewitched," said the captain wildly. "Stop!" he called out, recovering himself a little as the doctor bustled away to the steerage. "Stop! If it's true, Jolly, send her husband here aft to me. Damme, I'll have it out with one of the husbands!" said the captain, shaking his fist viciously at the empty air.

Ten minutes passed; and then there came staggering toward the captain, tottering this way and that with the rolling of the becalmed vessel, a long, lean, melancholy, light-haired man, with a Roman nose, a watery blue eye, and a complexion profusely spotted with large brown freckles. This was Simon Heavysides, the intelligent carpenter, with the wife and the family of seven small children on board.

"Oh! you're the man, are you?" said the captain.

The ship lurched heavily; and Simon Heavysides staggered away with a run to the opposite side of the deck, as if he preferred going straight overboard into the sea to answering the captain's question.

"You're the man — are you?" repeated the captain, following him, seizing him by the collar, and pinning him up fiercely against the bulwark. "It's your wife — is it? You infernal rascal! what do you mean by turning my ship into a lying-in hospital? You have committed an act of mutiny; or, if it isn't mutiny, it's next door to it. I've put a man in irons for less! I've more than half a mind to put *you* in irons! Hold up, you slippery lubber! What do you mean by bringing passengers I don't bargain for on board my vessel? What have you got to say for yourself, before I clap the irons on you?"

"Nothing, sir," answered Simon Heavysides, accepting the captain's strong language without a word of protest. "As for the punishment you mentioned just now, sir," continued Simon, "I wish to say — having seven children more than I know how to provide for, and an eighth coming to make things worse — I respectfully wish to say, sir, that my mind is in irons already; and I don't know as it will make much difference if you put my body in irons along with it."

The captain mechanically let go of

the carpenter's collar; the mild despair of the man melted him in spite of himself.

"Why did you come to sea? Why didn't you wait ashore till it was all over?" asked the captain, as sternly as he could.

"It's no use waiting, sir," remarked Simon. "In our line of life, as soon as it's over it begins again. There's no end to it that I can see," said the miserable carpenter, after a moment's meek consideration — "except the grave."

"Who's talking about the grave?" cried Mr. Jolly, coming up at that moment. "It's births we've got to do with on board this vessel — not burials. Captain Gillop, this woman, Mrs. Heavysides, can't be left in your crowded steerage in her present condition. She must be moved off into one of the empty berths — and the sooner the better, I can tell you."

The captain began to look savage again. A steerage passenger in one of his "state-rooms" was a nautical anomaly subversive of all discipline. He eyed the carpenter once more, as if he was mentally measuring him for a set of irons.

"I'm very sorry, sir," Simon remarked, politely, — "very sorry that any inadvertence of mine or Mrs. Heavysides —"

"Take your long carcass and your long tongue forward!" thundered the captain. "When talking will mend matters, I'll send for you again. Give your own orders, Jolly," he went on, resignedly, as Simon staggered off.

"Turn the ship into a nursery as soon as you like!"

Five minutes later — so expeditious was Mr. Jolly — Mrs. Heavysides appeared horizontally on deck, shrouded in blankets, and supported by three men. When this interesting procession passed the captain, he shrank aside from it with as vivid an appearance of horror as if a wild bull was being carried by him instead of a British matron.

The sleeping-berths below opened on either side out of the main cabin. On the left-hand side (looking toward the ship's bowsprit) was Mrs. Smallchild. On the right-hand side, opposite to her, the doctor established Mrs. Heavysides. A partition of canvas was next run up, entirely across the main cabin. The smaller of the two temporary rooms thus made lay nearest the stairs leading on deck, and was left free to the public. The larger was kept sacred to the doctor and his mysteries. When an old clothes-basket, emptied, cleaned, and comfortably lined with blankets (to serve for a make-shift cradle), had been in due course of time carried into the inner cabin, and had been placed midway between the two sleeping-berths, so as to be easily producible when wanted, the outward and visible preparations of Mr. Jolly were complete; the male passengers had all taken refuge on deck; and the doctor and the stewardess were left in undisturbed possession of the lower regions.

While it was still early in the afternoon the weather changed for the better. For once in a way, the wind came from a fair quarter, and the *Adventure* bowled along pleasantly before it almost on an even keel. Captain Gillop mixed with the little group of male passengers on the quarter-deck, restored to his sweetest temper; and set them his customary example, after dinner, of smoking a cigar.

"If this fine weather lasts, gentlemen," he said, "we shall make out very well with our meals up here, and we shall have our two small extra cabin passengers christened on dry land in a week's time, if their mothers approve of it. How do you feel in your mind, sir, about your good lady?"

Mr. Smallchild (to whom the inquiry was addressed) had his points of external personal resemblance to Simon Heavysides. He was neither so tall nor so lean, certainly; but he, too, had a Roman nose, and light hair, and watery blue eyes. With careful reference to his peculiar habits at sea, he had been placed conveniently close to the bulwark, and had been raised on a heap of old sails and cushions, so that he could easily get his head over the ship's side when occasion required. The food and drink which assisted in "restoring his tissue," when he was not asleep and not "squaring accounts with the sea," lay close to his hand. It was then a little after three o'clock; and the snore with which Mr. Smallchild answered the captain's inquiry showed that he had got round again, with the regularity of clock-work, to the period of the day when he recruited himself with sleep.

"What an insensible blockhead that man is!" said Mr. Sims, the middle-aged passenger, looking across the deck contemptuously at Mr. Smallchild.

"If the sea had the same effect on you that it has on him," retorted the invalid passenger, Mr. Purling, "you would just be as insensible yourself."

Mr. Purling (who was a man of sentiment) disagreed with Mr. Sims (who was a man of business) on every conceivable subject, all through the voyage. Before, however, they could continue the dispute about Mr. Smallchild, the doctor surprised them by appearing from the cabin.

"Any news from below, Jolly?" asked the captain, anxiously.

"None whatever," answered the doctor. "I've come to idle the afternoon away up here, along with the rest of you."

As events turned out, Mr. Jolly idled away an hour and a half exactly. At the end of that time Mrs. Drabble, the stewardess, appeared with a face of mystery, and whispered, nervously, to the doctor: —

"Please to step below directly, sir."

"Which of them is it?" asked Mr. Jolly.

"*Both* of them," answered Mrs. Drabble, emphatically.

The doctor looked grave; the stewardess looked frightened. The two immediately disappeared together.

"I suppose, gentlemen," said Captain Gillop, addressing Mr. Purling, Mr. Sims, and the first mate, who had just joined the party, — "I suppose it's only fit and proper, in the turn things have taken, to shake up Mr. Smallchild? And I don't doubt but what we ought to have the other husband handy, as a sort of polite attention under the circumstances. Pass the word forward there, for Simon Heavysides. Mr. Smallchild, sir! rouse up! Here's your good lady — Hang me, gentlemen, if I know exactly how to put it to him."

"Yes. Thank you," said Mr. Smallchild, opening his eyes drowsily. "Biscuit and cold bacon, as usual — when I'm ready. I'm not ready yet. Thank you. Good-afternoon." Mr. Smallchild closed his eyes again, and became, in the doctor's phrase, "totally comatose."

Before Captain Gillop could hit on any new plan for rousing this imperturbable passenger, Simon Heavysides once more approached the quarter-deck. "I spoke a little sharp to you, just now, my man," said the captain, "being worried in my mind by what's going on on board this vessel. But I'll make it up to you, never fear. Here's your wife in what they call an interesting situation. It's only right you should be within easy hail of her. I look upon you, Heavysides, as a steerage passenger in difficulties; and I freely give you leave to stop here along with us till it's all over."

"You are very good, sir," said Simon; "and I am indeed thankful to you and to these gentlemen. But please to remember, I have seven children already in the steerage — and there's nobody left to mind 'em but me. My wife has got over it uncommonly well, sir, on seven previous occasions — and I don't doubt but what she'll conduct herself in a similar manner on the eighth.

It will be a satisfaction to her mind, Captain Gillop and gentlemen, if she knows I'm out of the way, and minding the children. For which reason, I respectfully take my leave." With these words Simon made his bow, and returned to his family.

"Well, gentlemen, these two husbands take it easy enough, at any rate!" said the captain. "One of them is used to it, to be sure; and the other is —"

Here a banging of cabin doors below, and a hurrying of footsteps, startled the speaker and his audience into momentary silence and attention.

"Ease her with the helm, Williamson!" said Captain Gillop, addressing the man who was steering the vessel. "In my opinion, gentlemen, the less the ship pitches the better, in the turn things are taking now."

The afternoon wore on into evening, and evening into night.

Mr. Smallchild performed the daily ceremonies of his nautical existence as punctually as usual. He was aroused to a sense of Mrs. Smallchild's situation when he took his biscuit and bacon; lost the sense again when the time came round for "squaring his accounts;" recovered it in the interval which ensued before he went to sleep; lost it again, as a matter of course, when his eyes closed once more — and so on through the evening and early night. Simon Heavysides received messages occasionally (through the captain's care), telling him to keep his mind easy; returned messages mentioning that his mind was easy, and that the children were pretty quiet, but never approached the deck in his own person. Mr. Jolly now and then showed himself; said "All right! — no news;" took a little light refreshment, and disappeared again as cheerful as ever. The fair breeze still held; the captain's temper remained unruffled; the man at the helm eased the vessel, from time to time, with the most anxious consideration. Ten o'clock came; the moon rose and shone superbly; the nightly grog made its appearance on the quarter-deck; the captain gave the passengers the benefit of his company; and still nothing happened. Twenty minutes more of suspense slowly succeeded each other — and then, at last, Mr. Jolly was seen suddenly to ascend the cabin stairs.

To the amazement of the little group on the quarter-deck, the doctor held Mrs. Drabble, the stewardess, fast by the arm, and, without taking the slightest notice of the captain or the passengers, placed her on the nearest seat he could find. As he did this his face became visible in the moonlight, and displayed to the startled spectators an expression of blank consternation.

"Compose yourself, Mrs. Drabble," said the doctor, in tones of unmistakable alarm. "Keep quiet, and let the air blow over you. Collect yourself, ma'am — for Heaven's sake, collect yourself!"

Mrs. Drabble made no answer. She beat her hands vacantly on her knees, and stared straight before her, like a woman panic-stricken.

"What's wrong?" asked the captain, setting down his glass of grog in dismay. "Anything amiss with those two unfortunate women?"

"Nothing," said the doctor. "Both doing admirably well."

"Anything queer with their babies?" continued the captain. "Are there more than you bargained for, Jolly? Twins, for instance?"

"No! no!" replied Mr. Jolly, impatiently. "A baby apiece — both boys — both in first-rate condition. Judge for yourselves," added the doctor, as the two new cabin passengers tried their lungs below for the first time, and found that they answered their purpose in the most satisfactory manner.

"What the devil's amiss, then, with you and Mrs. Drabble?" persisted the captain, beginning to lose his temper again.

"Mrs. Drabble and I are two innocent people, and we have got into the most dreadful scrape that ever you heard of!" was Mr. Jolly's startling answer.

The captain, followed by Mr. Purling and Mr. Sims, approached the doctor with looks of horror. Even the man at the wheel stretched himself over it as far as he could to hear what was coming next. The only uninterested person present was Mr. Smallchild. His time had come round for going to sleep again, and he was snoring peacefully, with his biscuit and bacon close beside him.

"Let's hear the worst of it at once, Jolly," said the captain, a little impatiently.

The doctor paid no heed to his request. His whole attention was absorbed by Mrs. Drabble. "Are you better now, ma'am?" he asked anxiously.

"No better in my mind," answered Mrs. Drabble, beginning to beat her knees again. "Worse if anything."

"Listen to me," said Mr. Jolly, coaxingly. "I'll put the whole case over again to you, in a few plain questions. You'll find it all come back to your memory, if you only follow me attentively, and if you take time to think and collect yourself before you attempt to answer."

Mrs. Drabble bowed her head in speechless submission — and listened. Everybody else on the quarter-deck listened, except the impenetrable Mr. Smallchild.

"Now, ma'am!" said the doctor. "Our troubles began in Mrs. Heavyside's cabin, which is situated on the starboard side of the ship?"

"They did, sir," replied Mrs. Drabble.

"Good! We went backward and forward, an infinite number of times, between Mrs. Heavysides (starboard) and Mrs. Smallchild (larboard) — but we found that Mrs. Heavysides, having got the start, kept it — and when I called out, 'Mrs. Drabble! here's a chopping boy for you; come and take him!' — I called out starboard, didn't I?"

"Starboard, sir — I'll take my oath of it," said Mrs. Drabble.

"Good again! 'Here's a chopping boy,' I said. 'Take him, ma'am, and make him comfortable in the cradle.' And you took him, and made him comfortable in the cradle, accordingly. Now where was the cradle?"

"In the main cabin, sir," replied Mrs. Drabble.

"Just so! In the main cabin, because we hadn't got room for it in either of the sleeping-cabins. You put the starboard baby (otherwise Heavysides) in the clothes-basket cradle in the main cabin. Good once more. How was the cradle placed?"

"Crosswise to the ship, sir," said Mrs. Drabble.

"Crosswise to the ship? That is to say, with one side longwise toward the stern of the vessel, and one side longwise toward the bows. Bear that in mind — and now follow me a little further. No! no! don't say you can't, and your head's in a whirl. My next question will steady it. Carry your mind on half an hour, Mrs. Drabble. At the end of half an hour you heard my voice again; and my voice called out, 'Mrs. Drabble! here's another chopping boy for you; come and take him!' — and you came and took him larboard, didn't you?"

"Larboard, sir, I don't deny it," answered Mrs. Drabble.

"Better and better! 'Here is another chopping boy,' I said. 'Take him, ma'am, and make him comfortable in the cradle, along with number one.' And you took the larboard baby (otherwise Smallchild), and made him comfortable in the cradle along with the starboard baby (otherwise Heavysides), accordingly? Now what happened after that?"

"Don't ask me, sir!" exclaimed Mrs. Drabble, losing her self-control, and wringing her hands desperately.

"Steady, ma'am! I'll put it to you as plain as print. Steady! and listen to me. Just as you had made the larboard baby comfortable I had occasion to send you into the starboard (or Heavysides) cabin to fetch something which I wanted in the larboard (or Smallchild) cabin; I kept you there a little while along with me; I left you and went into the Heavy-sides cabin, and called to you to bring me something I wanted out of the Small-child cabin, but before you got half-way across the main cabin I said, 'No; stop where you are, and I'll come to you;' immediately after which Mrs. Smallchild alarmed you, and you came across to me of your own accord; and thereupon I stopped you in the main cabin, and said, 'Mrs. Drabble, your mind's getting confused; sit down and collect your scattered intellects;' and you sat down and tried to collect them ("And couldn't, sir," interposed Mrs. Drabble, parenthetically. "Oh, my head, my head!")

— "And tried to collect your scat-tered intellects, and couldn't?" con-tinued the doctor. "And the conse-quence was, when I came out from the Smallchild cabin to see how you were getting on, I found you with the clothes-basket cradle hoisted up on the cabin table, staring down at the babies inside, with your mouth dropped open, and both your hands twisted in your hair. And when I said, 'Anything wrong with either of those two fine boys, Mrs. Drabble?' you caught me by the coat-collar, and whispered in my right ear these words, 'Lord save us and help us, Mr. Jolly, I've confused the two babies in my mind, and I don't know which is which!"

"And I don't know now!" cried Mrs. Drabble, hysterically. "Oh, my head! my head! I don't know now!"

"Captain Gillop and gentlemen," said Mr. Jolly, wheeling round and addressing his audience with the com-posure of sheer despair, "that is the Scrape—and, if you ever heard of a worse one, I'll trouble you to compose this miserable woman by mentioning it immediately."

Captain Gillop looked at Mr. Purling and Mr. Sims. Mr. Purling and Mr. Sims looked at Captain Gillop. They were all three thunderstruck—and no wonder.

"Can't *you* throw any light on it, Jolly?" inquired the captain, who was the first to recover himself.

"If you knew what I have had to do below, you wouldn't ask me such a question as that," replied the doctor. "Remember that I have had the lives of two women and two children to an-swer for; remember that I have been cramped up in two small sleeping-cabins, with hardly room to turn round in, and just light enough from two mis-erable little lamps to see my hand be-fore me; remember the professional difficulties of the situation, the ship rolling about under me all the while, and the stewardess to compose into the bargain; bear all that in mind, will you, and then tell me, how much spare time I had on my hands for comparing two boys together inch by inch—two boys born at night, within half an hour of each other, on board a ship at sea. Ha, ha! I only wonder the mothers and the boys and the doctor are all five of them alive to tell the story!"

"No marks on one or other of them that happened to catch your eye?" asked Mr. Sims.

"They must have been strongish

marks to catch my eye in the light I had to work by, and in the professional difficulties I had to grapple with," said the doctor. "I saw they were both straight, well-formed children — and that's all I saw."

"Are their infant features sufficiently developed to indicate a family likeness?" inquired Mr. Purling. "Should you say they took after their fathers or their mothers?"

"Both of them have light eyes, and light hair — such as it is," replied Mr. Jolly, doggedly. "Judge for your-self."

"Mr. Smallchild has light eyes and light hair," remarked Mr. Sims.

"And Simon Heavysides has light eyes and light hair," rejoined Mr. Purling.

"I should recommend waking Mr. Smallchild, and sending for Heavysides, and letting the two fathers toss up for it," suggested Mr. Sims.

"The parental feeling is not to be trifled with in that heartless manner," retorted Mr. Purling. "I should recommend trying the Voice of Nature."

"What may that be, sir?" inquired Captain Gallop, with great curiosity.

"The maternal instinct," replied Mr. Purling. "The mother's intuitive knowledge of her own child."

"Ay, ay!" said the captain. "Well thought of. What do you say, Jolly, to the Voice of Nature?"

The doctor held up his hand impatiently. He was engaged in resuming the effort to rouse Mrs. Drabble's memory by a system of amateur cross-examination, with the unsatisfactory re-sult of confusing her more hopelessly than ever.

Could she put the cradle back, in her own mind, into its original position? No. Could she remember whether she laid the starboard baby (otherwise Heavysides) on the side of the cradle nearest the stern of the ship, or nearest the bows? No. Could she remember any better about the larboard baby (otherwise Smallchild)? No. Why did she move the cradle on to the cabin table, and so bewilder herself additionally, when she was puzzled already? Because it came over her, on a sudden, that she had forgotten, in the dreadful confusion of the time, which was which; and of course she wanted to look closer at them, and see; and she couldn't see; and to her dying day she should never forgive herself; and let them throw her overboard, for a miserable wretch, if they liked — and so on, till the persevering doctor was wearied out at last, and gave up Mrs. Drabble, and gave up, with her, the whole case.

"I see nothing for it but the Voice of Nature," said the captain, holding fast to Mr. Purling's idea. "Try it, Jolly — you can but try it."

"Something must be done," said the doctor. "I can't leave the women alone any longer, and the moment I get below they will both ask for their babies. Wait here till you're fit to be seen, Mrs. Drabble, and then follow me. Voice of Nature!" added Mr. Jolly, contemptuously, as he descended the cabin stairs. "Oh, yes, I'll try it — much good the Voice of Nature will do us, gentlemen. You shall judge for yourselves."

Favored by the night, Mr. Jolly cunningly turned down the dim lamps in the sleeping-cabins to a mere glimmer, on the pretext that the light was bad for his patients' eyes.. He then took up the first of the two unlucky babies that came to hand, marked the clothes in which it was wrapped with a blot of ink, and carried it in to Mrs. Smallchild, choosing her cabin merely because he happened to be nearest to it. The second baby (distinguished by having no mark) was taken by Mrs. Drabble to Mrs. Heavysides. For a certain time the two mothers and the two babies were left together. They were then separated again by medical order; and were afterward reunited, with the difference that the marked baby went on this occasion to Mrs. Heavysides, and the unmarked baby to Mrs. Smallchild — the result, in the obscurity of the sleeping-cabins, proving to be that one baby did just as well as the other, and that the Voice of Nature was (as Mr. Jolly had predicted) totally incompetent to settle the existing difficulty.

"While night serves us, Captain Gillop, we shall do very well," said the doctor, after he had duly reported the failure of Mr. Purling's suggested experiment. "But when morning comes, and daylight shows the difference between the children, we must be prepared with a course of some kind. If the two mothers below get the slightest suspicion of the case as it stands, the nervous shock of the discovery may do dreadful mischief. They must be kept deceived, in the interests of their own health. We must choose a baby for each of them when to-morrow comes, and then hold to the choice till the mothers are well and up again. The question is, who's to take the responsibility? I don't usually stick at trifles — but I candidly admit that I'm afraid of it."

"I decline meddling in the matter, on the ground that I am a perfect stranger," said Mr. Sims.

"And I object to interfere, from precisely similar motives," added Mr. Purling, agreeing for the first time with a proposition that emanated from his natural enemy all through the voyage.

"Wait a minute, gentlemen," said Captain Gillop. "I've got this difficult matter, as I think, in its right bearings. We must make a clean breast of it to the husbands, and let them take the responsibility."

"I believe they won't accept it," observed Mr. Sims.

"And I believe they will," asserted Mr. Purling, relapsing into his old habits.

"If they won't," said the captain, firmly, "I'm master on board this ship — and, as sure as my name is Thomas Gillop, I'll take the responsibility!"

This courageous declaration settled all difficulties for the time being; and a council was held to decide on future proceedings. It was resolved to remain passive until the next morning, on the last faint chance that a few hours' sleep might compose Mrs. Drabble's bewildered memory. The babies were to be moved into the main cabin before the daylight grew bright — or, in other words, before Mrs. Smallchild or Mrs. Heavysides could identify the infant who had passed the night with her. The doctor and the captain were to be assisted by Mr. Purling, Mr. Sims, and the first mate, in the capacity of witnesses; and the assembly so constituted was to meet, in consideration of the emergency of the case, at six o'clock in the morning, punctually.

At six o'clock, accordingly, with the weather fine, and the wind still fair, the proceedings began. For the last time Mr. Jolly cross-examined Mrs. Drabble, assisted by the captain, and supervised by the witnesses. Nothing whatever was elicited from the unfortunate stewardess. The doctor pronounced her confusion to be chronic, and the captain and the witnesses unanimously agreed with him.

The next experiment tried was the revelation of the true state of the case to the husbands.

Mr. Smallchild happened, on this occasion, to be "squaring his accounts" for the morning; and the first articulate words which escaped him in reply to the disclosure were, "Deviled biscuit and anchovy paste." Further perseverance merely elicited an impatient request that they would "pitch him overboard at once, and the two babies along with him." Serious remonstrance was tried next, with no better effect. "Settle it how you like," said Mr. Smallchild, faintly. "Do you leave it to me, sir, as commander of this vessel?" asked Captain Gillop. (No answer.) "Nod your head, sir, if you can't speak." Mr. Smallchild nodded his head roundwise on his pillow — and fell asleep. "Does that count for leave to me to act?" asked Captain Gillop of the witnesses. And the witnesses answered, decidedly, Yes.

The ceremony was then repeated with Simon Heavysides, who responded, as became so intelligent a man, with a proposal of his own for solving the difficulty.

"Captain Gillop and gentlemen," said the carpenter, with fluent and melancholy politeness, "I should wish to consider Mr. Smallchild before myself in this matter. I am quite willing to part with my baby (whichever he is); and I respectfully propose that Mr. Smallchild should take *both* the children, and so make quite sure that he has really got possession of his own son."

The only immediate objection to this ingenious proposition was started by the doctor, who sarcastically inquired of Simon, "what he thought Mrs. Heavysides would say to it?" The carpenter confessed that this consideration had escaped him, and that Mrs. Heavysides was only too likely to be an irremovable obstacle in the way of the proposed arrangement. The witnesses all thought so too; and Heavysides and his idea were dismissed together, after Simon had first gratefully expressed his entire readiness to leave it all to the captain.

"Very well, gentlemen," said Captain Gillop. "As commander on board, I reckon next after the husbands in the matter of responsibility. I have considered this difficulty in all its bearings, and I'm prepared to deal with it. The Voice of Nature (which you proposed, Mr. Purling) has been found to fail. The tossing up for it (which you proposed, Mr. Sims) doesn't square altogether with my notions of what's right in a very serious business. No, sir! I've got my own plan; and I'm now about to try it. Follow me below, gentlemen, to the steward's pantry."

The witnesses looked round on one another in the profoundest astonishment — and followed.

"Pickerel," said the captain, addressing the steward, " bring out the scales."

The scales were of the ordinary kitchen sort, with a tin tray on one side to hold the commodity to be weighed, and a stout iron slab on the other to support the weights. Pickerel placed these scales upon a neat little pantry table, fitted on the ball-and-socket principle, so as to save the breaking of crockery by swinging with the motion of the ship.

"Put a clean duster in the tray," said the captain. "Doctor,". he continued, when this had been done, " shut the doors of the sleeping-berths (for fear of the women hearing anything), and oblige me by bringing those two babies in·here."

"O sir!" exclaimed Mrs. Drabble, who had been peeping guiltily into the pantry — "oh, don't hurt the little dears! If anybody suffers, let it be me!"

"Hold your tongue, if you please, ma'am," said the captain. "And keep the secret of these proceedings, if you wish to keep your place. If the ladies ask for their children, say they will have them in ten minutes' time."

The doctor came in, and set down the clothes-basket cradle on the pantry floor. Captain Gillop immediately put on his spectacles, and closely examined the two unconscious innocents who lay beneath him.

"Six of one and half a dozen of the other," said the captain. "I don't see any difference between them. Wait a bit, though! Yes, I do. One's a bald baby. Very good. We'll begin with that one. Doctor, strip the bald baby, and put him in the scales."

The bald baby protested — in his own language — but in vain. In two minutes he was flat on his back in the tin tray, with the clean duster under him to take the chill off.

"Weigh him accurately, Pickerel," continued the captain. " Weigh him, if necessary, to an eighth of an ounce. Gentlemen! watch this proceeding closely; it's a very important one."

While the steward was weighing and the witnesses were watching, Captain Gillop asked his first mate for the log-book of the ship, and for pen and ink.

"How much, Pickerel?" asked the captain, opening the book.

"Seven pounds one ounce and a quarter," answered the steward.

"Right, gentlemen?" pursued the captain.

"Quite right," said the witnesses.

"Bald child — distinguished as Number One — weight, seven pounds one ounce and a quarter (avoirdupois)," repeated the captain, writing down the entry in the log-book. "Very good. We'll put the bald baby back now, doctor, and try the hairy one next."

The hairy one protested — also in his own language — and also in vain.

"How much, Pickerel?" asked the captain.

"Six pounds fourteen ounces and three-quarters," replied the steward.

" Right, gentlemen?" inquired the captain.

"Quite right," answered the witnesses.

" Hairy child — distinguished as Number Two — weight six pounds fourteen ounces and three-quarters (avoirdupois)," repeated and wrote the captain. " Much obliged to you, Jolly — that will do. When you have got the other baby back in the cradle, tell Mrs. Drabble neither of them must be taken out of it till further orders ; and then be so good as to join me and these gentlemen on deck. If anything of a discussion rises up among us, we won't run the risk of being heard in the sleeping-berths." With these words Captain Gillop led the way on deck, and the first mate followed with the log-book and the pen and ink.

" Now, gentlemen," began the captain, when the doctor had joined the assembly, " my first mate will open these proceedings by reading from the log a statement which I have written myself, respecting this business, from beginning to end. If you find it all equally correct with the statement of what the two children weigh, I'll trouble you to sign it, in your quality of witnesses, on the spot."

The first mate read the narrative, and the witnesses signed it, as perfectly correct. Captain Gillop then cleared his throat, and addressed his expectant audience in these words : —

" You'll all agree with me, gentlemen, that justice is justice, and that like must to like. Here's my ship of five hundred tons, fitted with her spars accordingly. Say she's a schooner of a hundred and fifty tons, the veriest landsman among you, in that case, wouldn't put such masts as these into her. Say, on the other hand, she's an Indiaman of a thousand tons, would our spars (excellent good sticks as they are, gentlemen) be suitable for a vessel of that capacity? Certainly not. A schooner's spars to a schooner, and a ship's spars to a ship, in fit and fair proportion."

Here the captain paused to let the opening of his speech sink well into the minds of the audience. The audience encouraged him with the parliamentary cry of " Hear! hear!" The captain went on : —

" In the serious difficulty which now besets us, gentlemen, I take my stand on the principle which I have just stated to you. And my decision is as follows : Let us give the heaviest of the two babies to the heaviest of the two women ; and let the lightest then fall, as a matter of course, to the other. In a week's time, if this weather holds, we shall all (please God) be in port ; and if there's a better way out of this mess than my way, the parsons and lawyers ashore may find it, and welcome."

With these words the captain closed his oration ; and the assembled council immediately sanctioned the proposal submitted to them, with all the unanimity of men who had no idea of their own to set up in opposition.

Mr. Jolly was next requested (as the only available authority) to settle the question of weight between Mrs. Smallchild and Mrs. Heavysides, and decided it without a moment's hesitation, in favor of the carpenter's wife, on the indisputable ground that she was the tallest and stoutest woman of the two. Thereupon the bald baby, "distinguished as Number One," was taken into Mrs. Heavysides's cabin; and the hairy baby, "distinguished as Number Two," was accorded to Mrs. Smallchild; the Voice of Nature, neither in the one case nor in the other, raising the slightest objection to the captain's principle of distribution. Before seven o'clock Mr. Jolly reported that the mothers and sons, larboard and starboard, were as happy and comfortable as any four people on board ship could possibly wish to be; and the captain thereupon dismissed the council with these parting remarks: —

"We'll get the studding-sails on the ship now, gentlemen, and make the best of our way to port. Breakfast, Pickerel, in half an hour, and plenty of it! I doubt if that unfortunate Mrs. Drabble has heard the last of this business yet. We must all lend a hand, gentlemen, and pull her through if we can. In other respects the job's over, so far as we are concerned; and the parsons and lawyers must settle it ashore."

The parsons and the lawyers did nothing of the sort, for the plain reason that nothing was to be done. In ten days the ship was in port, and the news was broken to the two mothers. Each one of the two adored her baby, after ten days' experience of it — and each one of the two was in Mrs. Drabble's condition of not knowing which was which.

Every test was tried. First, the test by the doctor, who only repeated what he had told the captain. Secondly, the test by personal resemblance; which failed in consequence of the light hair, blue eyes, and Roman noses shared in common by the fathers, and the light hair, blue eyes, and no noses worth mentioning shared in common by the children. Thirdly, the test of Mrs. Drabble, which began and ended in fierce talking on one side and floods of tears on the other. Fourthly, the test by legal decision, which broke down through the total absence of any instructions for the law to act on. Fifthly, and lastly, the test by appeal to the husbands, which fell to the ground in consequence of the husbands knowing nothing about the matter in hand. The captain's barbarous test by weight remained the test still — and here am I, a man of the lower order, without a penny to bless myself with, in consequence.

Yes! I was the bald baby of that memorable period. My excess in weight settled my destiny in life. The fathers and mothers on either side kept the babies according to the captain's principle of distribution, in despair of knowing what else to do. Mr. Smallchild, who was sharp enough when not seasick, made his fortune. Simon Heavysides persisted in increasing his family, and died in the work-house.

Judge for yourself (as Mr. Jolly might say) how the two boys born at sea fared in after-life. I, the bald baby, have seen nothing of the hairy baby for years past. He may be short, like Mr. Smallchild — but I happen to know that he is wonderfully like Heavy-sides, deceased, in the face. I may be tall, like the carpenter — but I have the Smallchild eyes, hair, and expression, notwithstanding. Make what you can of that! You will find it come, in the end, to the same thing. Smallchild, junior, prospers in the world, because he weighed six pounds, fourteen ounces and three-quarters. Heavysides, junior, fails in the world, because he weighed seven pounds one ounce and a quarter. Such is destiny, and such is life.- I'll never forgive *my* destiny as long as I live. There is my grievance. I wish you good-morning.

"BLOW UP WITH THE BRIG!"

A SAILOR'S STORY.

I HAVE got an alarming confession to make. I am haunted by a Ghost.

If you were to guess for a hundred years, you would never guess what my ghost is. I shall make you laugh to begin with — and afterward I shall make your flesh creep. My Ghost is the ghost of a Bedroom Candlestick.

Yes; a bedroom candlestick and candle, or a flat candlestick and candle — put it in which way you like — that is what haunts me. I wish it was something pleasanter and more out of the common way; a beautiful lady, or a mine of gold and silver, or a cellar of wine and a coach and horses, and such like. But, being what it is, I must take it for what it is, and make the best of it; and I shall thank you kindly if you will help me out by doing the same.

I am not a scholar myself, but I make bold to believe that the haunting of any man with anything under the sun begins with the frightening of him. At any rate, the haunting of me with a bedroom candlestick and candle began with the frightening of me with a bedroom candlestick and candle — the frightening of me half out of my life; and, for the time being, the frightening of me altogether out of my wits. That is not a very pleasant thing to confess before stating the particulars; but perhaps you will be the readier to believe that I am not a downright coward, because you find me bold enough to make a clean breast of it already, to my own great disadvantage so far.

Here are the particulars, as well as I can put them : —

I was apprenticed to the sea when I was about as tall as my own walking-stick; and I made good enough use of my time to be fit for a mate's berth at the age of twenty-five years.

It was in the year eighteen hundred and eighteen, or nineteen, I am not quite certain which, that I reached the before-mentioned age of twenty-five. You will please to excuse my memory not being very good for dates, names, numbers, places, and such like. No fear, though, about the particulars I have undertaken to tell you of; I have got them all ship-shape in my recollection; I can see them, at this moment, as clear as noonday in my own mind. But there is a mist over what went before, and, for the matter of that, a mist likewise over much that came after — and it's not very likely to lift at my time of life, is it?

Well, in eighteen hundred and eighteen, or nineteen, when there was peace in our part of the world — and not before it was wanted, you will say — there was fighting, of a certain scampering, scrambling kind, going on in that old battle-field which we seafaring men know by the name of the Spanish Main.

The possessions that belonged to the Spaniards in South America had broken into open mutiny and declared for themselves years before. There was plenty of bloodshed between the new government and the old; but the new had got the best of it, for the most part, under one General Bolivar — a famous man in his time, though he seems to have dropped out of people's memories now. Englishmen and Irishmen with a turn for fighting, and nothing particular to do at home, joined Bolivar as volunteers; and some of our merchants here found it a good venture to send supplies across the ocean to the popular side. There was risk enough, of course, in doing this; but where one speculation of the kind succeeded, it made up for two, at the least, that failed. And that's the true principle of trade, wherever I have met with it, all the world over.

Among the Englishmen who were concerned in this Spanish-American business, I, your humble servant, happened in a small way to be one.

I was then mate of a brig belonging to a certain firm in the city, which drove a sort of general trade, mostly in queer out-of-the-way places, as far from home as possible; and which freighted the brig, in the year I am speaking of, with a cargo of gunpowder for General Bolivar and his volunteers. Nobody knew anything about our instructions, when

we sailed, except the captain; and he didn't half seem to like them. I can't rightly say how many barrels of powder we had on board, or how much each barrel held — I only know we had no other cargo. The name of the brig was the *Good Intent* — a queer name enough, you will tell me, for a vessel laden with gunpowder, and sent to help a revolution. And as far as this particular voyage was concerned, so it was. I mean that for a joke, and I hope you will encourage me by laughing at it.

The *Good Intent* was the craziest old tub of a vessel I ever went to sea in, and the worst found in all respects. She was two hundred and thirty, or two hundred and eighty, tons burden, I forget which; and she had a crew of eight, all told — nothing like as many as we ought by rights to have had to work the brig. However, we were well and honestly paid our wages; and we had to set that against the chance of foundering at sea, and, on this occasion, likewise the chance of being blown up into the bargain.

In consideration of the nature of our cargo, we were harassed with new regulations, which we didn't at all like, relative to smoking our pipes and lighting our lanterns; and, as usual in such cases, the captain, who made the regulations, preached what he didn't practise. Not a man of us was allowed to have a bit of lighted candle in his hand when he went below — except the skipper; and he used his light, when he turned in, or when he looked over his charts on the cabin-table, just as usual.

This light was a common kitchen

candle or "dip," and it stood in an old battered flat candlestick, with all the japan worn and melted off, and all the tin showing through. It would have been more seaman-like and suitable in every respect if he had had a lamp or a lantern; but he stuck to his old candle-stick; and that same old candlestick has ever afterward stuck to *me*. That's another joke, if you please, and a bet-ter one than the first, in my opinion.

Well (I said "well" before, but it's a word that helps a man on like), we sailed in the brig, and shaped our course, first, for the Virgin Islands, in the West Indies; and, after sighting them, we made for the Leeward Islands next, and then stood on due south, till the look-out at the mast-head hailed the deck and said he saw land. That land was the coast of South America. We had had a wonderful voyage so far. We had lost none of our spars or sails, and not a man of us had been harassed to death at the pumps. It wasn't often the *Good Intent* made such a voyage as that, I can tell you.

I was sent aloft to make sure about the land, and I did make sure of it.

When I reported the same to the skipper, he went below, and had a look at his letter of instruction, and the chart. When he came on deck again, he altered our course a trifle to the eastward — I forget the point on the compass, but that don't matter. What I do remember is, that it was dark before we closed in with the land. We kept the lead going, and hove the brig to in from four to five fathoms water, or it might be six — I can't say for cer-tain. I kept a sharp eye to the drift of the vessel, none of us knowing how the currents ran on that coast. We all wondered why the skipper didn't anchor; but he said No, he must first show a light at the foretopmast-head, and wait for an answering light on shore. We did wait, and nothing of the sort appeared. It was starlight and calm. What little wind there was came in puffs off the land. I suppose we waited, drifting a little to the westward, as I made it out; the best part of an hour before anything happened — and then, instead of seeing the light on shore, we saw a boat com-ing toward us, rowed by two men only.

We hailed them, and they answered "Friends!" and hailed us by our name. They came on board. One of them was an Irishman, and the other was a coffee-colored native pilot, who jabbered a little English.

The Irishman handed a note to our skipper, who showed it to me. It in-formed us that the part of the coast we were off was not oversafe for discharg-ing our cargo, seeing that spies of the enemy (that is to say, of the old government) had been taken and shot in the neighborhood the day before. We might trust the brig to the native pilot; and he had his instructions to take us to another part of the coast. The note was signed by the proper parties; so we let the Irishman go back alone in the boat, and allowed the pilot to exercise his lawful authority over the brig. He kept us stretching off from the land till noon the next day — his instructions, seemingly, ordering him to keep us well out of sight of the shore. We only altered our course in the afternoon, so as to close in with the land again a little before midnight.

This same pilot was about as ill-looking a vagabond as ever I saw; a skinny, cowardly, quarrelsome mongrel, who swore at the men in the vilest broken English, till they were every one of them ready to pitch him overboard. The skipper kept them quiet, and I kept them quiet; for the pilot being given us by our instructions, we were bound to make the best of him. Near night-fall, however, with the best will in the world to avoid it, I was unlucky enough to quarrel with him.

He wanted to go below with his pipe, and I stopped him, of course, because it was contrary to orders. Upon that he tried to hustle by me, and I put him away with my hand. I never meant to push him down; but somehow I did. He picked himself up as quick as lightning, and pulled out his knife. I snatched it out of his hand, slapped his murderous face for him, and threw his weapon overboard. He gave me one ugly look, and walked aft. I didn't think much of the look then, but I remembered it a little too well afterward.

We were close in with the land again, just as the wind failed us, between eleven and twelve that night, and dropped our anchor by the pilot's directions.

It was pitch-dark, and a dead, airless calm. The skipper was on deck, with two of our best men for watch. The rest were below, except the pilot, who coiled himself up, more like a snake than a man, on the forecastle. It was not my watch till four in the morning. But I didn't like the look of the night, or the pilot, or the state of things generally, and I shook myself down on deck to get my nap there, and be ready for any thing at a moment's notice. The last I remember was the skipper whispering to me that he didn't like the look of things either, and that he would go below and consult his instructions again. That is the last I remember, before the slow, heavy, regular roll of the old brig on the groundswell rocked me off to sleep.

I was awoke by a scuffle on the forecastle and a gag in my mouth. There was a man on my breast and a man on my legs, and I was bound hand and foot in half a minute.

The brig was in the hands of the Spaniards. They were swarming all over her. I heard six heavy splashes in the water, one after another. I saw the captain stabbed to the heart as he came running up the companion, and I heard a seventh splash in the water. Except myself, every soul of us on board had been murdered and thrown into the sea. Why I was left, I couldn't think, till I saw the pilot stoop over me with a lantern and look, to make sure of who I was. There was a devilish grin on his face, and he nodded his head at me, as much as to say, *You* were the man who hustled me down and slapped my face, and I mean to play the game of cat and mouse with you in return for it!

I could neither move nor speak, but I could see the Spaniards take off the main hatch and rig the purchases for getting up the cargo. A quarter of an hour afterward I heard the sweeps of a schooner, or other small vessel, in the water. The strange craft was laid alongside of us, and the Spaniards set to work to discharge our cargo into her. They all worked hard except the pilot; and he came from time to time, with his lantern, to have another look at me, and to grin and nod always in the same devilish way. I am old enough now not to be ashamed of confessing the truth, and I don't mind acknowledging that the pilot frightened me. .

The fright, and the bonds, and the gag, and the not being able to stir hand or foot, had pretty nigh worn me out by the time the Spaniards gave over work. This was just as the dawn broke. They had shifted a good part of our cargo on board their vessel, but nothing like all of it, and they were sharp enough to be off with what they had got before daylight.

I need hardly say that I had made up my mind by this time to the worst I could think of. The pilot, it was clear enough, was one of the spies of the enemy, who had wormed himself into the confidence of our consignees without being suspected. He, or more likely his employers, had got knowledge enough of us to suspect what our cargo was; we had been anchored for the night in the safest berth for them to surprise us in; and we had paid the penalty of having a small crew, and consequently an insufficient watch. All this was clear enough — but what did the pilot mean to do with *me?*

On the word of a man, it makes my flesh creep now only to tell you what he did with me. .

After all the rest of them were out of the brig, except the pilot and two Spanish seamen, these last took me up, bound and gagged as I was, lowered me into the hold of the vessel, and laid me along on the floor, lashing me to it with ropes' ends, so that I could just turn from one side to the other, but could not roll myself fairly over, so as to change my place. They then left me. Both of them were the worse for liquor; but the devil of a pilot was sober — mind that! — as sober as I am at the present moment. .

I lay in the dark for a little while, with my heart thumping as if it was going to jump out of me. I lay about five minutes or so when the pilot came down into the hold alone.

He had the captain's cursed flat candlestick and a carpenter's awl in one hand, and a long, thin twist of cotton-yarn, well oiled, in the other. He put the candlestick, with a new " dip " candle lighted in it, down on the floor about two feet from my face, and close against the side of the vessel. The light was feeble enough; but it was sufficient to show a dozen barrels of gunpowder or more left all round me in the hold of the brig. I began to suspect what he was after the moment I noticed the barrels. The horrors laid hold of me from head to foot, and the sweat poured off my face like water.

I saw him go next to one of the barrels of powder standing against the side of the vessel in a line with the candle, and about three feet, or rather better, away from it. He bored a hole in the side of the barrel with his awl, and the horrid powder came trickling out, as black as hell, and dripped into the hollow of his hand, which he held to catch it. When he had got a good handful, he stopped up the hole by jamming one end of his oiled twist of cotton-yarn fast into it and he then rubbed the powder into the whole length of the yarn till he had blackened every hair-breadth of it.

The next thing he did — as true as I sit here, as true as the heaven above us all — the next thing he did was to carry the free end of his long, lean, black, frightful slow-match to the lighted candle alongside my face. He tied it (the bloody-minded villain!) in several folds round the tallow dip, about a third of the distance down, measuring from the flame of the wick to the lip of the candlestick. He did that; he looked to see that my lashings were all safe; and then he put his face close to mine, and whispered in my ear, "Blow up with the brig!"

He was on deck again the moment after, and he and the two others shoved the hatch on over me. At the farthest end from where I lay they had not fitted it down quite true, and I saw a blink of daylight glimmering in when I looked in that direction. I heard the sweeps of the schooner fall into the water — splash! splash! fainter and fainter, as they swept the vessel out in the dead calm, to be ready for the wind in the offing. Fainter and fainter, splash, splash! for a quarter of an hour or more.

While those sounds were in my ears, my eyes were fixed on the candle.

It had been freshly lighted. If left to itself, it would burn for between six and seven hours. The slow-match was twisted round it about a third of the way down, and therefore the flame would be about two hours reaching it. There I lay, gagged, bound, lashed to the floor; seeing my own life burning down with the candle by my side — there I lay, alone on the sea, doomed to be blown to atoms, and to see that doom drawing on, nearer and nearer with every fresh second of time, through nigh on two hours to come; powerless to help myself, and speechless to call for help to others. The wonder to me is that I didn't cheat the flame, the slow-match, and the powder, and die of the horror of my situation before my first half-hour was out in the hold of the brig.

I can't exactly say how long I kept the command of my senses after I had ceased to hear the splash of the schooner's sweeps in the water. I can trace back everything I did and everything I thought, up to a certain point; but, once past that, I get all abroad, and lose myself in my memory now, much as I lost myself in my own feelings at the time.

The moment the hatch was covered over me, I began, as every other man would have begun in my place, with a frantic effort to free my hands. In the mad panic I was in, I cut my flesh with the lashings as if they had been knife-blades, but I never started them. There was less chance still of freeing my legs, or of tearing myself from the fastenings that held me to the floor. I gave in when I was all but suffocated for want of breath. The gag, you will please to remember, was a terrible enemy to me; I could only breathe freely through my nose — and that is but a poor vent when a man is straining his strength as far as ever it will go.

I gave in and lay quiet, and got my breath again, my eyes glaring and straining at the candle all the time.

While I was staring at it, the notion struck me of trying to blow out the flame by pumping a long breath at it suddenly through my nostrils. It was too high above me, and too far away from me, to be reached in that fashion. I tried, and tried, and tried ; and then I gave in again, and lay quiet again, always with my eyes glaring at the candle, and the candle glaring at *me*. The splash of the schooner's sweeps was very faint by this time. I could only just hear them in the morning stillness. Splash! splash! — fainter and fainter — splash! splash!

Without exactly feeling my mind going, I began to feel it getting queer as early as this. The snuff of the candle was growing taller and taller, and the length of tallow between the flame and the slow-match, which was the length of my life, was getting shorter and shorter. I calculated that I had rather less than an hour and a half to live.

An hour and a half! Was there a chance in that time of a boat pulling off to the brig from shore? Whether the land near which the vessel was anchored was in possession of our side, or in possession of the enemy's side, I made out that they must, sooner or later, send to hail the brig merely because she was a stranger in those parts. The question for *me* was, how soon? The sun had not risen yet, as I could tell by looking through the chink in the hatch. There was no coast village near us, as we all knew, before the brig was seized, by seeing no lights on shore. There was no wind, as I could tell by listening, to bring any strange vessel near. 'If I had had six hours to live, there might have been a chance for me, reckoning from sunrise to noon. But with an hour and a half, which had dwindled to an hour and a quarter by this time — or in other words, with the earliness of the morning, the uninhabited coast, and the dead calm all against me — there was not the ghost of a chance. As I felt that, I had another struggle — the last — with my bonds, and only cut myself the deeper for my pains.

I gave in once more, and lay quiet, and listened for the splash of the sweeps.

Gone! Not a sound could I hear but the blowing of the fish now and then on the surface of the sea, and the creak of the brig's crazy old spars, as she rolled gently from side to side with the little swell there was on the quiet water.

An hour and a quarter. The wick grew terribly as the quarter slipped away, and the charred top of it began to thicken and spread out mushroom-shape. It would fall off soon. Would it fall off red-hot, and would the swing of the brig cant it over the side of the candle and let it down on the slow-match? If it would I had about ten minutes to live instead of an hour.

This discovery set my mind for a minute on a new tack altogether. I began to ponder with myself what sort of a death blowing up might be. Painful! Well, it would be, surely, too sudden for that. Perhaps just one crash inside me, or outside me, or both; and nothing more! Perhaps not even a crash; that and death and the scattering of this living body of mine into millions of fiery sparks, might all happen in the same instant! I couldn't make it out; I couldn't settle how it would be. The minute of calmness in my mind left it before I had half done thinking; and I got all abroad again.

When I came back to my thoughts, or when they came back to me (I can't say which), the wick was awfully tall, the flame was burning with a smoke above it, the charred top was broad and red, and heavily spreading out to its fall.

My despair and horror at seeing it took me in a new way, which was good and right, at any rate, for my poor soul. I tried to pray — in my own heart, you will understand, for the gag put all lip-praying out of my power. I tried, but the candle seemed to burn it up in me. I struggled hard to force my eyes from the slow, murdering flame, and to look up through the chink in the hatch at the blessed daylight. I tried once, tried twice; and gave it up. I next tried only to shut my eyes, and keep them shut — once — twice — and the second time I did it. "God bless old mother, and sister Lizzie! God keep them both, and forgive me!" That was all I had time to say, in my own heart, before my eyes opened again, in spite of me, and the flame of the candle flew into them, flew all over me, and burned up the rest of my thoughts in an instant.

I couldn't hear the fish blowing now; I couldn't hear the creak of the spars; I couldn't think; I couldn't feel the sweat of my own death agony on my face — I could only look at the heavy, charred top of the wick. It swelled, tottered, bent over to one side, dropped — red-hot at the moment of its fall — black and harmless, even before the swing of the brig had canted it over into the bottom of the candlestick.

I caught myself laughing.

Yes! laughing at the safe fall of the bit of wick. But for the gag, I should have screamed with laughing. As it was, I shook with it inside me — shook till the blood was in my head, and I was all but suffocated for want of breath. I had just sense enough left to feel that my own horrid laughter at that awful moment was a sign of my brain going at last. I had just sense enough left to make another struggle before my mind broke loose like a frightened horse, and ran away with me.

One comforting look at the blink of daylight through the hatch was what I tried for once more. The fight to force my eyes from the candle and to get that one look at the daylight was the hardest I had had yet; and I lost the fight. The flame had hold of my eyes as fast as the lashings had hold of my hands. I couldn't look away from it. I couldn't even shut my eyes, when I tried that next, for the second time. There was the wick growing tall once more. There was the space of unburned candle between the light and the slow-match shortened to an inch or less.

How much life did that inch leave me? Three-quarters of an hour? Half an hour? Fifty minutes? Twenty minutes? Steady! an inch of tallow-candle would burn longer than twenty minutes. An inch of tallow! the notion of a man's body and soul being kept together by an inch of tallow! Wonderful! Why, the greatest king that sits on a throne can't keep a man's body and soul together; and here's an inch of tallow that can do what the king can't! There's something to tell mother when I get home, which will surprise her more than all the rest of my voyages put together. I laughed inwardly again at the thought of that, and shook and swelled and suffocated myself, till the light of the candle leaped in through my eyes, and licked up the laughter, and burned it out of me, and made me all empty and cold and quiet once more.

Mother and Lizzie. I don't know when they came back; but they did come back — not, as it seemed to me, into my mind this time, but right down bodily before me, in the hold of the brig.

Yes; sure enough, there was Lizzie, just as light-hearted as usual, laughing at me. Laughing? Well, why not? Who is to blame Lizzie for thinking I'm lying on my back, drunk in the cellar, with the beer-barrels all around me? Steady! she's crying now — spinning round and round in a fiery mist, wringing her hands, screeching out for help — fainter and fainter, like the splash of the schooner's sweeps. Gone — burned up in the fiery mist! Mist? fire? no; neither one nor the other. It's mother makes the light — mother knitting, with ten flaming points at the ends of her fingers and thumbs, and slow-matches hanging in bunches all round her face instead of her own gray hair. Mother in her old arm-chair, and the pilot's long skinny hands hanging over the back of the chair, dripping with gunpowder. No! no gunpowder, no chair, no mother — nothing but the pilot's face, shining red-hot, like a sun, in the fiery mist; turning upside down in the fiery mist; running backward and forward along the slow-match, in the fiery mist; spinning millions of miles in a minute, in the fiery mist — spinning itself smaller and smaller into one tiny point; and that point darting on a sudden straight into my head — and then, all fire and all mist — no hearing, no seeing, no thinking, no feeling — the brig, the sea, my own self, the whole world, all gone together!

After what I've just told you, I know nothing and remember nothing, till I woke up (as it seemed to me) in a comfortable bed, with two rough-and-ready men like myself sitting on each side of my pillow, and a gentleman standing watching me at the foot of the bed. It was about seven in the morning. My sleep (or what seemed like my sleep to me) had lasted better than eight months — I was among my own countrymen in the island of Trinidad — the men at each side of my pillow were my keepers, turn and turn about — and the gentleman standing at the foot of the bed was the doctor. What I said and did in those eight months, I have never known, and never shall. I woke out of it as if it had been one long sleep — that's all I know.

It was another two months or more before the doctor thought it safe to answer the questions I asked him.

The brig had been anchored, just as I had supposed, off a part of the coast which was lonely enough to make the Spaniards pretty sure of no interruption, so long as they managed their murderous work quietly under cover of night.

My life had not been saved·from the shore, but from the sea. An American vessel, becalmed in the offing, had made out the brig as the sun rose; and the captain, having his time on his hands in consequence of the calm, and seeing a vessel anchored where no vessel had any reason to·be,·had manned one of his boats, and sent his mate with it, to look a little closer into the matter, and bring back a report of what he saw.

What he saw, when he and his men found the brig deserted and boarded her, was a gleam of candle-light through the chink in the hatchway. The flame was within about a thread's breadth of the slow-match when he lowered himself into the hold; and if he had not had the sense and coolness to cut the match in two with his knife before he touched the candle, he and his men might have been blown up along wita the brig as well as me. The match caught, and turned into spluttering red fire, in the very act of putting the candle out; and if the communication with the powder-barrel had not been cut off, the Lord only knows what might have happened.

What became of the Spanish schooner and the pilot, I have never heard from that day to this.

As for the brig, the Yankees took. her, as they took me, to Trinidad, and claimed their salvage, and got it, I hope, for their own sakes. I was landed just in the same state as when they rescued me from the brig — that is to say, clean out of my senses. But please to remember, it was a long time ago; and, take my word for it, I was discharged cured, as I have told you. Bless your hearts, I'm all right now, as you may see. I'm a little. shaken by telling the story, as is only natural — a little shaken, my good friends, that's all.

THE QUEEN'S REVENGE.

THE name of Gustavus Adolphus, the faithful Protestant, the great general, and the good king of Sweden, has been long since rendered familiar to English readers of history. We all know how this renowned warrior and monarch was beloved by his soldiers and subjects, how successfully he fought through a long and terrible war, and how nobly he died on the field of battle. With his death, however, the interest of the English reader in Swedish affairs seems to terminate. Those who have followed the narrative of his life carefully to the end, may remember that he left behind him an only child, a daughter named Christina. But of the character of this child, and of her extraordinary adventures after she grew to womanhood, the public in England is, for the most part, entirely ignorant. In the popular historical and romantic literature of France, Queen Christina is a notorious character. In the literature of this country she has, hitherto, been allowed but little chance of making her way to the notice of the world at large.

And yet the life of this woman was in itself a romance. At six years old she was Queen of Sweden, with the famous Oxenstiern for guardian. This great and good man governed the kingdom in her name until she had lived through her minority. Four years after her coronation she, of her own accord, abdicated her rights in favor of her cousin, Charles Gustavus. Young and beautiful, the most learned and most accomplished woman of her time, she resolutely turned her back on the throne of her inheritance, and set forth to wander through civilized Europe in the character of an independent traveller who was resolved to see all varieties of men and manners, to collect all the knowledge which the widest experience could give her, and to measure her mind boldly against the greatest minds of the age.

So far, the interest excited by her character and her adventures is of the most picturesquely attractive kind. There is something strikingly new in the spectacle of a young queen who prefers the pursuit of knowledge to the possession of a throne, and who barters a royal birthright for the privilege of being free. Unhappily, the portrait of Christina cannot be painted throughout in bright colors only. It must be recorded to her disgrace that, when her travels brought her to Rome, she abandoned the religion for which her father fought and died. And it must be admitted in the interests of truth, that she freed herself from other restraints beside the restraint of royalty. Mentally distinguished by her capacities, she was morally degraded by her vices and her crimes.

The events in the strange life of Christina, especially those connected with her actions in the character of a Queen-Errant, present ample materials for a biography, which might be regarded in England as a new contribution to our historical literature. One among the many extraordinary adventures which marked the Queen's wandering career, may be related in these pages as an episode in the history of her life which is complete in itself. The events of which the narrative is composed, throw light, in many ways, on the manners, habits and opinions of a past age ; and they can, moreover, be presented in the remarkable words of an eye-witness who beheld them two centuries ago.

The scene is the palace of Fontainebleau ; the time is the close of the year sixteen hundred and fifty-seven ; the persons are the wandering Queen Christina ; her grand equerry the Marquis Monaldeschi ; and Father Le Bel of the convent of Fontainebleau, the witness whose testimony we are shortly about to cite.

Monaldeschi, as his name implies, was an Italian by birth. He was a handsome,. accomplished man, refined in his manners, supple in his disposition, and possessed of the art of making himself eminently agreeable in the society of women. With these personal recommendations, he soon won his way to the favor of Queen Christina. Out of the long list of her lovers, not one of the many whom she encouraged caught so long and firm a hold of her capricious fancy as Monaldeschi. The intimacy between them probably took its rise, on her side at least, in as deep a sincerity of affection as it was in Christina's nature to feel. On the side of the Italian, the connection was prompted solely ·by ambition. As soon as he had reaped all the advantages of the position of chief favorite in the Queen's court, he wearied of his royal mistress, and addressed his attentions secretly to a young Roman lady, whose youth and beauty powerfully attracted him, and whose fatal influence over his actions ultimately led to his ruin and his death.

After endeavoring to ingratiate himself with the Roman lady, in various ways, Monaldeschi found that the surest means of winning her favor lay in satisfying her malicious curiosity on the subject of the secret frailties of Queen Christina. He was not a man to be troubled by any scrupulous feelings of honor when the interests of his own intrigues happened to be concerned ; and he shamelessly took advantage of the position that he held towards Christina, to commit breaches of confidence of the most meanly infamous kind. Not contented with placing in the possession of the Roman lady the series of the Queen's letters to himself, containing secrets that she had revealed to him in the fullest confidence of his worthiness to be trusted, he wrote letters of his own to the new object of his addresses, in which he ridiculed Christina's fondness for him, and sarcastically described her smallest personal defects with a heartless effrontery which the most patient of women would have found it impossible to forgive. While he was thus privately betraying the confidence that had been reposed in him, he was publicly affecting the most unalterable attachment and the most sincere respect for the Queen.

For some time this disgraceful deception proceeded successfully. But the hour of the discovery was at hand, and the instrument of effecting it was a certain cardinal who was desirous of supplanting Monaldeschi in the Queen's favor. The priest contrived to get possession of the whole correspondence, which had been privately confided to the Roman lady, including, besides Christina's letters, the letters which Monaldeschi had written in ridicule of his royal mistress. The whole collection of documents was enclosed by the cardinal in one packet, and was presented by him, at a private audience, to the Queen.

It is at this critical point of the story that the testimony of the eye-witness whom we propose to quote, begins. Father Le Bel was present at the terrible execution of the Queen's vengeance on Monaldeschi, and was furnished with copies of the whole correspondence which had been abstracted from the Roman lady. Having been trusted with the secret, he is wisely and honorably silent throughout his narrative on the subject of Monaldeschi's offence. Such particulars of the Italian's baseness and ingratitude as have been presented here have been gathered from the contradictory reports which were current at the time, and which have been preserved by the old French collectors of historical anecdotes. The details of the extraordinary punishment of Monaldeschi's offence, which are now to follow, may be given in the words of Father Le Bel himself. The reader will understand that his narrative begins immediately after Christina's discovery of the perfidy of her favorite.

The sixth of November, sixteen hundred and fifty-seven (writes Father Le Bel), at a quarter past nine in the morning, Queen Christina of Sweden, being at that time lodged in the royal palace of Fontainebleau, sent one of her men-servants to my convent, to obtain an interview with me. The messenger, on being admitted to my presence, inquired if I was the superior of the convent, and when I replied in the affirmative, informed me that I was expected to present myself immediately before the Queen of Sweden.

Fearful of keeping her majesty waiting, I followed the man at once to the palace, without waiting to take any of my brethren from the convent with me.

After a little delay in the antechamber, I was shown into the Queen's room. She was alone; and I saw by the expression of her face, as I respectfully begged to be favored with her commands, that something was wrong. She hesitated for a moment; and then told me, rather sharply, to follow her to a place where she might speak with the certainty of not being overheard. She led me into the Galerie des Cerfs, and, turning round on me suddenly, asked if we had ever met before. I informed her Majesty that I had once had the honor of presenting my respects to her; that she had received me graciously, and that there the interview had ended. She nodded her head and looked about her a little; then said, very abruptly, that I wore a dress (referring to my convent costume) which encouraged her to put perfect faith in my honor; and she desired me to promise beforehand that I would keep the secret with which she was about to entrust me as strictly as if I had heard it in the confessional. I answered, respectfully, that it was part of my sacred profession to be trusted with secrets; that I had never betrayed the private affairs of any one; and that I could answer for myself as worthy to be honored by the confidence of a queen.

Upon this, her Majesty handed me a packet of papers, sealed in three places, but having no superscription of any sort. She ordered me to keep it under lock and key, and to be prepared to give it her back again before any person in whose presence she might see fit to ask me for it. She, further, charged me to remember the day, the hour, and the place in which she had given me the packet; and with that last piece of advice she dismissed me. I left her alone in the gallery, walking slowly away from me, with her head drooping on her bosom, and her mind, as well

as I could presume to judge, perturbed by anxious thoughts.*

On Saturday, the tenth of November, at one o'clock in the afternoon, I was sent for to the palace again. I took the packet out of my private cabinet, feeling that I might be asked for it; and then followed the messenger as before. This time he led me at once to the Galerie des Cerfs. The moment I entered it, he shut the door behind me with such extraordinary haste and violence, that I felt a little startled. As soon as I recovered myself, I saw her Majesty standing in the middle of the gallery, talking to one of the gentlemen of her court, who was generally known by the name of The Marquis, and whom I soon ascertained to be the Marquis Monaldeschi, Grand Equerry of the Queen of Sweden. I approached her Majesty and made my bow — then stood before her, waiting until she should think proper to address me.

With a stern look on her face, and with a loud, clear, steady voice, she asked me, before the Marquis and before three other men who were also in the gallery, for the packet which she had confided to my care.

As she made that demand, two of the three men moved back a few paces, while the third, the captain of her guard, advanced rather nearer to her. I handed her back the packet. She looked at it thoughtfully for a little

* Although Father Le Bel discreetly abstains from mentioning the fact, it seems clear from the context that he was permitted to read, and that he did read, the papers contained in the packet.

while; then opened it, and took out the letters and written papers which it contained, handing them to the Marquis Monaldeschi, and insisting on his reading them. When he had obeyed, she asked him, with the same stern look and the same steady voice, whether he had any knowledge of the documents which he had just been reading. The Marquis turned deadly pale, and answered that he had now read the papers referred to for the first time.

"Do you deny all knowledge of them?" said the Queen. "Answer me plainly, sir. Yes or no?"

The Marquis turned paler still. "I deny all knowledge of them," he said, in faint tones, with his eyes on the ground.

"Do you deny all knowledge of these too?" said the Queen, suddenly producing a second packet of manuscript from under her dress, and thrusting it in the Marquis's face.

He started, drew back a little, and answered not a word. The packet which the Queen had given to me contained copies only. The original papers were those she had just thrust in the Marquis's face.

"Do you deny your own seal and your own handwriting?" she asked.

He murmured a few words, acknowledging both the seal and the handwriting to be his own, and added some phrases of excuse, in which he endeavored to cast the blame that attached to the writing of the letters on the shoulders of other persons. While he was speaking, the three men in attendance on the Queen silently closed around him.

Her Majesty heard him to the end. "You are a traitor," she said, and turned her back on him.

The three men, as she spoke these words, drew their swords.

The Marquis heard the clash of the blades against the scabbards, and, looking quickly round, saw the drawn swords behind him. He caught the Queen by the arm immediately, and drew her away with him, first into one corner of the gallery, then into another, entreating her in the most moving terms to listen to him, and to believe in the sincerity of his repentance. The Queen let him go on talking without showing the least sign of anger or impatience. Her color never changed; the stern look never left her countenance. There was something awful in the clear, cold, deadly resolution which her eyes expressed while they rested on the Marquis's face.

At last she shook herself free from his grasp, still without betraying the slightest irritation. The three men with the drawn swords, who had followed the Marquis silently, as he led the Queen from corner to corner of the gallery, now closed round him again, as soon as he was left standing alone.

There was perfect silence for a minute or more. Then the Queen addressed herself to me.

"Father le Bel," she said, "I charge you to bear witness that I treat this man with the strictest impartiality." She pointed, while she spoke, to the Marquis Monaldeschi with a little ebony riding-whip that she carried in her hand. "I offer that worthless traitor all the time he requires — more time than he has any right to ask for — to justify himself if he can."

The Marquis, hearing these words, took some letters from a place of concealment in his dress, and gave them to the Queen, along with a small bunch of keys. He snatched these last from his pocket so quickly, that he drew out with them a few small silver coins which fell to the floor. As he addressed himself to the Queen again, she made a sign with her ebony riding-whip to the men with the drawn swords; and they retired toward one of the windows of the gallery. I, on my side, withdrew out of hearing. The conference which ensued between the Queen and the Marquis lasted nearly an hour. When it was over, her Majesty beckoned the men back again with the whip, and then approached the place where I was standing.

"Father le Bel," she said, in her clear, ringing, resolute tones, "there is no need for me to remain here any longer. I leave that man," she pointed to the Marquis again, "to your care. Do all that you can for the good of his soul. He has failed to justify himself, and I doom him to die."

If I had heard sentence pronounced against myself, I could hardly have been more terrified than I was when the Queen uttered these last words. The Marquis heard them where he was standing, and flung himself at her feet. I dropped on my knees by his side, and entreated her to pardon him, or, at least, to visit his offence with some milder punishment than the punishment of death.

"I have said the words," she answered, addressing herself only to me; "and no power under Heaven shall make me unsay them. Many a man has been broken alive on the wheel for offences which were innocence itself compared with the offence which this perjured traitor has committed against me. I have trusted him as I might have trusted a brother; he has infamously betrayed that trust; and I exercise my royal rights over the life of a traitor. Say no more to me. I tell you again, he is doomed to die."

With those words the Queen quitted the gallery, and left me alone with Monaldeschi and the three executioners, who were waiting to kill him.

The unhappy man dropped on his knees at my feet, imploring me to follow the Queen, and make one more effort to obtain his pardon. Before I could answer a word, the three men surrounded him, held the points of their swords to his sides — without, however, actually touching him — and angrily recommended him to make his confession to me, without wasting any more time. I entreated them, with the tears in my eyes, to wait as long as they could, so as to give the Queen time to reflect, and, perhaps, to falter in her deadly intentions toward the Marquis. I succeeded in producing such an impression on the chief of the three men, that he left us, to obtain an interview with the Queen, and to ascertain if there was any change in her purpose. After a very short absence he came back, shaking his head.

"There is no hope for you," he said, addressing Monaldeschi. "Make your peace with Heaven. Prepare yourself to die!"

"Go to the Queen!" cried the Marquis, kneeling before me with clasped hands. "Go to the Queen yourself; make one more effort to save me. O Father le Bel, run one more risk — venture one last entreaty — before you leave me to die!"

"Will you wait till I come back?" I said to the three men.

"We will wait," they answered, and lowered their sword-points to the ground.

I found the Queen alone in her room, without the slightest appearance of agitation in her face or her manner. Nothing that I could say had the slightest effect on her. I adjured her by all that religion holds most sacred, to remember that the noblest privilege of any sovereign is the privilege of granting mercy; that the first of Christian duties is the duty of forgiving. She heard me unmoved. Seeing that entreaties were thrown away, I ventured, at my own proper hazard, on reminding her that she was not living now in her own kingdom of Sweden, but that she was the guest of the King of France, and lodged in one of his own palaces; and I boldly asked her if she had calculated the possible consequence of authorizing the killing of one of her attendants inside the walls of Fontainebleau, without any preliminary form of trial, or any official notification of the offence that he had committed. She answered me coldly, that it was enough that she knew the unpardonable nature of the offence of which Monaldeschi had been guilty; that she stood in a perfectly independent position toward the King of France; that she was absolute mistress of her own actions, at all times and in all places; and that she was accountable to nobody under Heaven for her conduct toward her subjects and servants, over whose lives and liberties she possessed sovereign rights, which no consideration whatever should induce her to resign.

Fearful, as I was, of irritating her, I still ventured on reiterating my remonstrances. She cut them short by hastily signing to me to leave her.

As she dismissed me, I thought I saw a slight change pass over her face; and it occurred to me that she might not have been indisposed at that moment to grant some respite, if she could have done so without appearing to falter in her resolution, and without running the risk of letting Monaldeschi escape her. Before I passed the door, I attempted to take advantage of the disposition to relent which I fancied I had perceived in her; but she angrily reiterated the gesture of dismissal before I had spoken half-a-dozen words. With a heavy heart, I yielded to necessity, and left her.

On returning to the gallery, I found the three men standing round the Marquis, with their sword-points on the floor, exactly as I had left them.

"Is he to live or to die?" they asked when I came in.

There was no need for me to reply in words; my face answered the question. The Marquis groaned heavily, but said nothing. I sat myself down on a stool, and beckoned to him to come to me, and begged him, as well as my terror and wretchedness would let me, to think of repentance, and to prepare for another world. He began his confession kneeling at my feet, with his head on my knees. After continuing it for some time, he suddenly started to his feet with a scream of terror. I contrived to quiet him, and to fix his thoughts again on heavenly things. He completed his confession, speaking sometimes in Latin, sometimes in French, sometimes in Italian, according as he could best explain himself in the agitation which now possessed him.

Just as he had concluded, the Queen's chaplain entered the gallery. Without waiting to receive absolution, the unhappy Marquis rushed away from me to the chaplain, and, still clinging desperately to the hope of life, besought him to intercede with the Queen. The two talked together in low tones, holding each other by the hand. When their conference was over, the chaplain left the gallery again, taking with him the chief of the three executioners who were appointed to carry out the Queen's deadly purpose. After a short absence, this man returned without the chaplain. "Get your absolution," he said briefly to the Marquis, "and make up your mind to die."

Saying these words, he seized Monaldeschi; pressed him back against the wall at the end of the gallery, just under the picture of Saint Germain; and, before I could interfere, or even turn aside from the sight, struck at the Marquis's right side with his sword. Monaldeschi caught the blade with his hand, cutting three of his fingers in the act. At the same moment, the point touched his side and glanced off. Upon this, the man who had struck at him exclaimed, "He has armor under his clothes," and, at the same moment, stabbed Monaldeschi in the face. As he received the wound, he turned round toward me, and cried out loudly, "Father le Bel! Father le Bel!"

I advanced toward him immediately. As I did so, the man who had wounded him retired a little, and signed to his two companions to withdraw also. The Marquis, with one knee on the ground, asked pardon of God, and said certain last words in my ear. I immediately gave him absolution, telling him that he must atone for his sins by suffering death, and that he must pardon those who were about to kill him. Having heard my words, he flung himself forward on the floor. While he was falling, one of the three executioners who had not assailed him as yet, struck at his head, and wounded him on the surface of the skull.

The Marquis sank on his face; then raised himself a little, and signed to the men to kill him outright, by striking him on the neck. The same man who had last wounded him, obeyed by cutting two or three times at his neck, without, however, doing him any great injury. For it was indeed true that he wore armor under his clothes, which armor consisted of a shirt of mail, weighing nine or ten pounds, and rising so high round his neck, inside his collar, as to defend it successfully from any chance blow with a sword.

Seeing this, I came forward to exhort the Marquis to bear his sufferings with patience, for the remission of his sins. While I was speaking, the chief of the three executioners advanced, and asked me if I did not think it was time to give Monaldeschi the finishing stroke. I pushed the man violently away from me, saying that I had no advice to offer on the matter, and telling him that if I had any orders to give, they would be for the sparing of the Marquis's life, and not for the hastening of his death. Hearing me speak in those terms, the man asked my pardon, and confessed that he had done wrong in addressing me on the subject at all.

He had hardly finished making his excuses to me, when the door of the gallery opened. The unhappy Marquis, hearing the sound, raised himself from the floor, and, seeing that the person who entered was the Queen's chaplain, dragged himself along the gallery, holding on by the tapestry that hung from the walls, until he reached the feet of the holy man. There he whispered a few words (as if he was confessing) to the chaplain, who, after first asking my permission, gave him absolution, and then returned to the Queen.

As the chaplain closed the door, the man who had struck the Marquis on the neck, stabbed him adroitly with a long, narrow sword in the throat, just above the edge of the shirt of mail. Monaldeschi sank on his right side, and spoke no more. For a quarter of an hour longer he still breathed, during which time I prayed by him, and exhorted him as I best could. When the bleeding from this last wound ceased, his life ceased with it. It was then a quarter to four o'clock. The death agony of the miserable man had lasted, from the time of the Queen's first pronouncing sentence on him, for nearly three hours.

I said the De Profundis over his body. While I was praying, the three men sheathed their swords, and the chief of them rifled the Marquis's pockets. Finding nothing on him but a prayer-book and a small knife, the chief beckoned to his companions, and they all three marched to the door in silence, went out, and left me alone with the corpse.

A few minutes afterward I followed them to go and report what had happened to the Queen.

I thought her color changed a little when I told her that Monaldeschi was dead; but those cold, clear eyes of hers never softened, and her voice was still as steady and firm as when I first heard its tones on entering the gallery that day. She spoke very little, only saying to herself, " He is dead, and he deserved to die!" Then, turning to me, she added, " Father, I leave the care of burying him to you; and, for my own part, I will charge myself with the expense of having masses enough said for the repose of his soul." I ordered the body to be placed in a coffin, which I instructed the bearers to remove to the church-yard on a tumbril, in consequence of the great weight of the corpse, of the misty rain that was falling, and of the bad state of the roads. On Monday, the twelfth of November, at a quarter to six in the evening, the Marquis was buried in the parish church of Avon, near the font of holy water. The next day, the Queen sent one hundred livres, by two of her servants, for masses for the repose of his soul.

Thus ends the extraordinary narrative of Father Le Bel. It is satisfactory to record, as some evidence of the progress of humanity, that this barbarous murder, which would have passed unnoticed in the feudal times, as an ordinary and legitimate exercise of a sovereign's authority over a vassal, excited, in the middle of the seventeenth century, the utmost disgust and horror throughout Paris. The prime minister at that period, Cardinal Mazarin (by no means an over-scrupulous man, as all readers of French history know), wrote officially to Christina, informing her that "a crime so atrocious as that which had just been committed under her sanction, in the Palace of Fontainebleau, must be considered as a sufficient cause for banishing the Queen of Sweden from the court and dominions of his sovereign, who, in common with every honest man in the kingdom, felt horrified at the lawless outrage which had just been committed on the soil of France."

To this letter Queen Christina sent the following answer, which, as a specimen of spiteful effrontery, has probably never been matched: —

"MONSIEUR MAZARIN, — Those who have communicated to you the details of the death of my equerry, Monaldeschi, knew nothing at all about it. I think it highly absurd that you should have compromised so many people for the sake of informing yourself about one simple fact. Such a proceeding on your part, ridiculous as it is, does not, however, much astonish me. What I am amazed at is, that you and the king, your master, should have dared to express disapproval of what I have done.

"Understand, all of you — servants and masters, little people and great — that it was my sovereign pleasure to act as I did. I neither owe, nor render, an account of my actions to any one — least of all to a bully like you.

* * * * * *

"It may be well for you to know, and to report to any one whom you can get to listen to you, that Christina cares little for your court, and less still for you. When I want to revenge myself, I have no need of your formidable power to help me. My honor obliged me to act as I did; my will is my law, and you ought to know how to respect it. Understand, if you please, that wherever I choose to live, there I am Queen; and that the men about me, rascals as they may be, are better than you and the ragamuffins whom you keep in your service.

* * * * * *

"Take my advice, Mazarin, and behave yourself for the future so as to merit my favor; you cannot, for your own sake, be too anxious to deserve it. Heaven preserve you from venturing on any more disparaging remarks about my conduct! I shall hear of them, if I am at the other end of the world, for I have friends and followers in my service who are as unscrupulous and as vigilant as any in yours, though it is probable enough that they are not quite so heavily bribed."

After replying to the prime minister of France in these terms, Christina was wise enough to leave the kingdom immediately.

For three years more she pursued her travels. At the expiration of that time her cousin, the King of Sweden, in whose favor she had abdicated, died. She returned at once to her own country, with the object of possessing herself once more of the royal power. Here the punishment of the merciless crime that she had sanctioned overtook her at last. The brave and honest people of Sweden refused to be governed by the woman who had ordered the murder of Monaldeschi, and who had forsaken the national religion for which her father had died. Threatened with the loss of her revenues as well as the loss of her sovereignty, if she remained in Sweden, the proud and merciless Christina yielded for the first time in her life. She resigned once more all right and title to the royal dignity, and left her native country for the last time. The final place of her retirement is Rome. She died there in the year sixteen hundred and eighty-nine. Even in the epitaph which she ordered to be placed on her tomb, the strange and daring character of the woman breaks out. The whole record of that wild and wicked existence was summoned up with stern brevity in this one line : —

CHRISTINA LIVED SEVENTY–TWO YEARS.

FRAGMENTS OF PERSONAL EXPERIENCE.

MY BLACK MIRROR.

HAS everybody heard of Doctor Dee, the magician, and of the black speculum or mirror of cannel-coal, in which he could see at will everything in the wide world, and many things beyond it? If so, I may introduce myself to my readers in the easiest manner possible. Although I cannot claim to be a descendant of Doctor Dee, I profess the occult art to the extent of keeping a black mirror, made exactly after the model of that possessed by the old astrologer. My speculum, like his, is constructed of an oval piece of cannel-coal, highly polished, and set on a wooden back, with a handle to hold it by. Nothing can be simpler than its appearance; nothing more marvellous than its capacities — provided always that the person using it be a true adept. Any man who disbelieves nothing is a true adept. Let him get a piece of cannel-coal, polish it highly, clean it before use with a white cambric handkerchief, retire to a private sitting-room, invoke the name of Doctor Dee, shut both eyes for a moment, and open them again suddenly on the black mirror. If he does not see anything he likes, after that — past, present, or future — then let him depend on it there is some speck or flaw of incredulity in his nature; and the sad termination of his career may be considered certain. Sooner or later he will end in being nothing but a rational man.

I, who have not one morsel of rationality about me; I, who am as true an adept as if I had lived in the good old times ("the Ages of Faith," as another adept has very properly called them), find unceasing interest and occupation in my black mirror. For everything I want to know, and for everything I want to do, I consult it. This very day, for instance (being in the position of most of the other inhabitants of London at the present season), I am thinking of soon going out of town. My time for being away is so limited, and my wanderings have extended, at home and abroad, in so many directions, that I can hardly hope to visit any really beautiful scenes, or gather any really interesting experiences that are absolutely new to me. I must go to some place that I have visited before; and I must, in common regard to my own holiday interests, take care that it is a place where I have already thoroughly enjoyed myself, without a single drawback to my pleasure that is worth mentioning.

Under these circumstances, if I were a mere rational man, what should I do? Weary my memory to help me to decide on a destination, by giving me my past travelling recollections in one long panorama — although I can tell by experience that of all my faculties memory is the least serviceable at the very time when I most want to employ it. As a true adept, I know better than to give myself any useless trouble of this sort. I retire to my private sitting-room, take up my black mirror, mention what I want — and, behold! on the surface of the cannel-coal the image of my former travels passes before me, in succession of dream-scenes. I revive my past experiences, and I make my present choice out of them, by the evidence of my own eyes; and I may add, by that of my own ears also — for the figures in my magic landscapes move and speak.

Shall I go on the Continent again? Yes. To what part of it? Suppose I revisit Austrian Italy, for the sake of renewing my familiarity with certain views, buildings, and pictures which once delighted me? But let me first ascertain whether I had any serious drawbacks to complain of on making acquaintance with that part of the world. Black mirror! show me my first evening in Austrian Italy.

A cloud rises on the magic surface — rests on it a little while — slowly disappears. My eyes are fixed on the cannel-coal. I see nothing, hear nothing, of the world about me. The first of the magic scenes grows visible. I behold it, as in a dream. Away with the ignorant Present! I am in Italy again.

The darkness is just coming on. I see myself looking out of the side window of a carriage. The hollow roll of the wheels has changed to a sharp rattle, and we have entered a town. We cross a vast square, illuminated by two lamps and a glimmer of reflected light from a coffee-shop window. We get on into a long street, with heavy stone arcades for foot-passengers to walk under. Everything looks dark and confused; grim visions of cloaked men flit by, all smoking; shrill female voices rise above the clatter of our wheels, and then subside again in a moment. We stop. The bells on the horses' necks ring their last tiny peal for the night. A greasy hand opens the carriage door, and helps me down the steps. I am under an archway, with blank darkness before me, with a smiling man holding a flaming tallow-candle by my side, with street spectators silently looking on behind me. They wear high-crowned hats and brown cloaks, mysteriously muffling them up to the chin. Brigands, evidently. Pass, Scene! I am a peaceable man, and I don't like the suspicion of a stiletto, even in a dream.

Show me my sitting-room. Where did I dine, and how, on my first evening in Austrian Italy?

I am in the presence of two cheerful waiters, with two flaring candles. One is lighting lamps; the other is setting brush-wood and logs in a blaze in a perfect cavern of a hearth. Where am I, now that there is plenty of light to see by? Apparently in a banqueting-hall, fifty feet long by forty wide. This is my private sitting-room, and I am to eat my little bit of dinner in it all alone. Let me look about observantly while the meal is preparing. Above me is an arched painted ceiling, all alive with Cupids rolling about on clouds, and scattering perpetual roses on the heads of travellers beneath. Around me are classical landscapes of the school which treats the spectator to umbrella-shaped trees, calm green oceans, and foregrounds rampant with dancing goddesses. Beneath me is something elastic to tread upon, smelling very like old straw, which indeed it is, covered with a thin drugget. This is humanely intended to protect me against the cold of the stone or brick floor, and is a concession to English prejudices on the subject of comfort. May I be grateful for it, and take no unfriendly notice of the fleas, though they are crawling up my legs from the straw and the drugget already!

What do I see next? Dinner on table. Drab-colored soup, which will take a great deal of thickening with grated Parmesan cheese, and five dishes all around it. Trout fried in oil, rolled beef steeped in succulent brown gravy, roast chicken with water-cresses, square pastry cakes with mince-meat inside them, fried potatoes — all excellent. This is really good Italian cookery; it is more fanciful than the English, and more solid than the French. It is not greasy, and none of the fried dishes taste in the slightest degree of lamp-oil. The wine is good, too — effervescent, smacking of the Muscatel grape, and only eighteen-pence a

bottle. The second course more than sustains the character of the first. Small browned birds that look like larks, their plump breasts clothed succulently with a counterpane of fat bacon, their tender backs reposing on beds of savory toast — stewed pigeon — a sponge-cake pudding — baked pears. Where could one find a better dinner or a pleasanter waiter to serve at table? He is neither servile nor familiar, and is always ready to occupy any superfluous attention I have to spare with all the small-talk that is in him. He has, in fact, but one fault, and that consists in his very vexatious and unaccountable manner of varying the language in which he communicates with me.

I speak French and Italian, and he can speak French also as well as his own tongue. I naturally, however, choose Italian on first addressing him, because it is his native language. He understands what I say to him perfectly, but he answers me in French. I bethink myself, upon this, that he may be wishing, like the rest of us, to show off any little morsel of learning he has picked up, or that he may fancy I understand French better than I do Italian, and may be politely anxious to make our colloquy as easy as possible to me. Accordingly I humor him, and change to French when I next speak. No sooner are the words out of my mouth than, with inexplicable perversity, he answers me in Italian. All through the dinner I try hard to make him talk the same language that I do, yet, excepting now and then a few insignificant phrases, I never succeed.

What is the meaning of his playing this game of philological seesaw with me? Do the people here actually carry the national politeness so far as to flatter the stranger by according him an undisturbed monopoly of the language in which he chooses to talk to them? I can not explain it, and dessert surprises me in the midst of my perplexities. Four dishes again! Parmesan cheese, macaroons, pears, and green figs. With these and another bottle of the effervescent wine, how brightly the evening will pass away by the blazing wood-fire! Surely I can do no better than to go to Austrian Italy again, after having met with such a first welcome to the country as this. Shall I put down the cannel-coal, and determine without any more ado on paying a second visit to the land that is cheered by my comfortable inn? No, not too hastily. Let me try the effect of one or two more scenes from my past travelling experience in this particular division of the Italian peninsula before I decide.

Black Mirror! how did I end my evening at the comfortable inn?

The cloud passes again, heavily and thickly this time, over the surface of the mirror — clears away slowly — shows me myself dozing luxuriously by the red embers with an empty bottle at my side. A suddenly opening door wakes me up; the landlord of the inn approaches, places a long, official-looking book on the table, and hands me pen and ink. I inquire peevishly what I am wanted to write at that time of night, when I am just digesting my dinner. The landlord answers respectfully that I am required to give the police a full, true, and particular account of myself. I approach the table, thinking this demand rather absurd, for my passport is already in the hands of the authorities. However, as I am in a despotic country, I keep my thoughts to myself open a blank page in the official-looking book, see that it is divided into columns, with printed headings, and find that I no more understand what they mean than I understand an assessed tax-paper at home, to which, by-the-by, the blank page bears a striking general resemblance. The headings are technical official words, which I now meet with as parts of Italian speech for the first time. I am obliged to appeal to the polite landlord, and, by his assistance, I get gradually to understand what it is the Austrian police want of me.

The police require to know, before they will let me go on peaceably tomorrow, first, What is my name in full? (Answered easily enough.) Second, What is my nation? (British, and delighted to cast it in the teeth of continental tyrants.) Third, Where was I born? (In London — parish of Marylebone — and I wish my native vestry knew how the Austrian authorities were using me.) Fourth, Where do I live? (In London, again — and I have half a mind to write to the *Times* about this nuisance before I go to bed.) Fifth, How old am I? (My age is what it has been for the last seven years, and what it will remain till further notice — twenty-five exactly.) What next? By all that is inquisitive, here are the police wanting to know

(Sixth) whether I am married or single! Landlord, what is the Italian for Bachelor? "Write Nubile, signor." Nubile? That means Marriageble. Permit me to remark, my good sir, that this is a woman's definition of a ·bachelor, not a man's. No matter, let it pass. What next? (Oh, distrustful despots! what next?) Seventh, What is my condition? (First-rate condition, to be sure, — full of rolled beef, toasted larks, and effervescent wine. Condition! What do they mean by that? Profession, is it? I have not got one. What shall I write? "Write Proprietor, signor." Very well; but I don't know that I am proprietor of anything except the clothes I stand up in; even my trunk was borrowed from a friend.) Eighth, Where do I come from? Ninth, Where am I going to? Tenth, When did I get my passport? Eleventh, Where did I get my passport? Twelfth, Who gave me my passport? Was there ever such a monstrous string of questions to address to a harmless, idle man, who only wants to potter about Italy quietly in a post-chaise? Do they catch Mazzini, landlord, with all these precautions? No; they only catch me. There! there! take your Travellers' Book back to the police. Surely, such unfounded distrust of my character as the production of that volume at my dinner-table implies, forms a serious drawback to the pleasure of travelling in Austrian Italy. Shall I give up at once all idea of going there in my own innocent character, again? No; let me be deliberate at arriving at a decision; let me patiently try the experiment of looking at one more scene from the past.

Black Mirror! how did I travel in Austrian Italy after I had paid my bill in the morning, and had left my comfortable inn?

The new dream-scene shows me evening again. I have joined another English traveller in taking a vehicle that they called a calèche. It is a frowzy kind of sedan-chair on wheels, with greasy leather curtains and cushions. In the days of its prosperity and youth it might have been a state coach, and might have carried Sir Robert Walpole to court, or the Abbé Dubois to a supper with the Regent Orleans. It is driven by a tall, cadaverous, ruffianly postilion, with his clothes all in rags, and without a spark of mercy for his miserable horses. It smells badly, looks badly, goes badly; and jerks, and cracks, and totters as if it would break down altogether — when it is suddenly stopped on a rough stone pavement in front of a lonely post-house, just as the sun is sinking and the night is setting in.

The postmaster comes out to superintend the harnessing of fresh horses. He is tipsy, familiar, and confidential; he first apostrophizes the calèche with contemptuous curses, then takes me mysteriously aside, and declares that the whole high-road onward to our morning's destination swarms with thieves. It seems, then, that the Austrian police reserve all their vigilance for innocent travellers; and leave local rogues entirely unmolested. I make this reflection, and ask the postmaster what he recommends us to do for the protection of our portmanteaus, which are tied on the roof of the calèche. He answers that, unless we take special precautions, the thieves will get up behind, on our crazy foot-board, and will cut the trunks off the top of our frowzy travelling-carriage, under cover of the night, while we are quietly seated inside, seeing and expecting nothing. We instantly express our readiness to take any precautions that any one may be kind enough to suggest. The postmaster winks, lays his finger archly on the side of his nose, and gives an unintelligible order in the patois of the district. Before I have time to ask what he is going to do, every idler about the post-house who can climb scales the summit of the calèche, and every idler who cannot stands roaring and gesticulating below with a lighted candle in his hand.

While the hubbub is at its loudest, a rival travelling-carriage suddenly drives into the midst of us, in the shape of a huge barrel-organ on wheels, and bursts out awfully in the darkness with the grand march in "Semiramide," played with the utmost fury of the drum, cymbal, and trumpet-stops. The noise is so bewildering that my travelling companion and I take refuge inside our carriage, and shut our eyes, and stop our ears, and abandon ourselves to despair. After a time, our elbows are jogged, and a string apiece is given to us through each window. We are informed in shouts, accompanied fiercely by the grand march, that the strings are fastened to our portmanteaus above; that we are to keep the loose ends round our forefingers all night, and the moment we feel a tug, we may be quite certain the thieves are at work, and may feel justified in stopping the carriage and fighting for our baggage without any more ado. Under these agreeable auspices, we start again, with our strings round our forefingers. We feel like men about to ring the bell — or like men engaged in deep-sea fishing — or like men on the point of pulling the string of a shower-bath. Fifty times at least, during the next stage, each of us is certain that he feels a tug, and pops his head agitatedly out of the window, and sees absolutely nothing, and falls back again exhausted with excitement in a corner of the calèche. All through the night this wear and tear of our nerves goes on; and all through the night (thanks, probably, to the ceaseless popping of our heads out of the windows) not the ghost of a thief comes near us. We begin, at last, almost to feel that it would be a relief to be robbed — almost to doubt the policy of resisting any mercifully larcenous hands stretched forth to rescue us from the incubus of our own baggage. The morning dawn finds us languid and haggard, with the accursed portmanteau strings dangling unregarded in the bottom of the calèche. And this is taking our pleasure! This is an incident of travel in Austrian Italy! Faithful Black Mirror, accept my thanks. The warning of the two last dream-scenes that you have shown me shall not be disregarded. Whatever other direction I may take, when I go out of town for the present season, one road at least I know that I shall avoid — the road that leads to Austrian Italy.

Shall I keep on the northern side of the Alps, and travel a little, let us say, in German Switzerland? Black Mirror! how did I get on when I was last in that country? Did I like my introductory experience at my first inn?

The vision changes, and takes me again to the outside of a house of public entertainment; a great white, clean, smooth-fronted, opulent-looking hotel, — a very different building from my dingy, cavernous Italian inn. At the street door stands the landlord. He is a little, lean, rosy man, dressed all in black, and looking like a master-undertaker. I observe that he neither steps forward nor smiles when I get out of the carriage and ask for a bedroom. He gives me the shortest possible answer, growls guttural instructions to a waiter, then looks out into the street again, and, before I have so much as turned my back on him, forgets my existence immediately. The vision changes again, and takes me inside the hotel. I am following a waiter upstairs; the man looks unaffectedly sorry to see me. In the bedroom corridor we find a chambermaid asleep, with her head on a table. She is woke up; opens a door with a groan, and scowls at me reproachfully when I say that the room will do. I descend to dinner. Two waiters attend on me, under protest, and look as if they were on the point of giving warning every time I require them to change my plate. At the second course the landlord comes in, and stands and stares at me intently and silently with his hands in his pockets. This may be his way of seeing that my dinner is well served; but it looks much more like his way of seeing that I do not abstract any spoons from his table. I become irritated by the boorish staring and frown-

ing of everybody about me, and express myself strongly on the subject of my reception at the hotel to an English traveller dining near me.

The English traveller is one of those exasperating men who are always ready to put up with injuries, and he coolly accounts for the behavior of which I complain, by telling me that it is the result of the blunt honesty of the natives, who cannot pretend to take an interest in me which they do not really feel. What do I care about the feelings of the stolid landlord and the sulky waiters? I require the comforting outward show from them, — the inward substance is not of the smallest consequence to me. When I travel in civilized countries, I want such a reception at my inn as shall genially amuse and gently tickle all the region round about my organ of self-esteem. Blunt honesty, which is too offensively truthful to pretend to be glad to see me, shows no corresponding integrity — as my own experience informs me at this very hotel — about the capacities of its winebottles, but gives me a pint and charges me for a quart in the bill, like the rest of the world. Blunt honesty, although it is too brutally sincere to look civilly distressed and sympathetic when I say that I am tired after my journey, does not hesitate to warm up, and present before me as newly dressed, a Methuselah of a duck that has been cooked several times over, several days ago, and paid for, though not eaten, by my travelling predecessors. Blunt honesty fleeces me according to every established predatory law of the landlord's code, yet shrinks from the amiable duplicity of fawning affectionately before me all the way upstairs when I first present myself to be swindled. Away with such detestable sincerity as this! Away with the honesty which brutalizes a landlord's manners without reforming his bottles or his bills! Away with my German-Swiss hotel, and the extortionate cynic who keeps it! Let others pay tribute if they will to that boor in innkeeper's clothing, the color of my money he shall never see again.

Suppose I avoid German Switzerland, and try Switzerland Proper? Mirror! how did I travel when I last found myself on the Swiss side of the Alps?

The new vision removes me even from the most distant view of a hotel of any kind, and places me in a wild mountain country where the end of a rough road is lost in the dry bed of a torrent. I am seated in a queer little box on wheels, called a Char, drawn by a mule and a mare, and driven by a jovial coachman in a blue blouse. I have hardly time to look down alarmedly at the dry bed of the torrent, before the Char plunges into it. Rapidly and recklessly we thump along over rocks and stones, acclivities and declivities that would shake down the stoutest English travelling-carriage, knock up the best-bred English horses, nonplus the most knowing English coachman. Jovial Blue Blouse, singing like a nightingale, drives ahead regardless of every obstacle; the mule and mare tear along as if the journey was the great enjoyment of the day to them; the Char cracks, rends, sways, bumps, and totters, but scorns, as becomes a hardy little mountain vehicle, to over-turn or come to pieces. When we are not among the rocks we are rolling and heaving in sloughs of black mud and sand, like a Dutch herring-boat in a groundswell. It is all one to Blue Blouse and the mule and mare. They are just as ready to drag through sloughs as to jolt over rocks; and when we do come occasionally to a bit of unencumbered ground, they always indemnify themselves for past hardship and fatigue by galloping like mad. As for my own sensations in the character of passenger in the Char, they are not, physically speaking, of the pleasantest possible kind. I can only keep myself inside my vehicle by dint of holding tight with both hands by anything I can find to grasp at; and I am so shaken throughout my whole anatomy that my very jaws clatter again, and my feet play a perpetual tattoo on the bottom of the Char. Did I hit on no method of travelling more composed and deliberate than this, I wonder, when I was last in Switzerland? Must I make up my mind to be half shaken to pieces if I am bold enough to venture on going there again?

The surface of the Black Mirror is once more clouded over. It clears, and the vision is now of a path along the side of a precipice. A mule is following the path, and I am the adventurous traveller who is astride on the beast's back. The first observation that occurs to me in my new position is, that mules thoroughly deserve their reputation for obstinacy, and that, in regard to the particular animal on which I am riding, the less I interfere with him, and the more I conduct myself as if I was a pack-saddle on his back, the better we are sure to get on together.

Carrying pack-saddles is his main business in life; and though he saw me get on his back, he persists in treating me as if I was bale of goods, by walking on the extreme edge of the precipice, so as not to run any risk of rubbing his load against the safe, or mountain, side of the path. In this and in other things I find that he is the victim of routine, and the slave of habit. He has a way of stopping short, placing himself in a slanting position, and falling into a profound meditation at some of the most awkward turns in the wild mountain roads. I imagine at first that he may be halting in this abrupt and inconvenient manner to take breath; but then he never exerts himself so as to tax his lungs in the smallest degree, and he stops on the most unreasonable, irregular principles, sometimes twice in ten minutes — sometimes not more than twice in two hours, — evidently just as his new ideas happen to absorb his attention or not. It is part of his exasperating character at these times always to become immersed in reflection where the muleteer's staff has not room to reach him with the smallest effect; and where, loading him with blows being out of the question, loading him with abusive language is the only other available process for getting him on. I find that he generally turns out to be susceptible to the influence of injurious epithets after he has heard himself insulted five or six times. Once his obdurate nature gives way, even at the third appeal. He has just stopped with me on his back, to amuse himself, at a dangerous part of the road, with a little hard thinking in a steeply slanting position; and it becomes, therefore, urgently necessary to abuse him into proceeding forthwith. First, the muleteer calls him a Serpent, — he never stirs an inch. Secondly, the muleteer calls him Frog, — he goes on, imperturbably, with his meditation. Thirdly, the muleteer roars out indignantly, *Ah sacré nom d'un Butor!* (which, interpreted by the help of my Anglo-French dictionary, means apparently, Ah, sacred name of a Muddle-head!); and at this extraordinary adjuration the beast instantly jerks up his nose, shakes his ears, and goes on his way indignantly.

Mule-riding, under these circumstances, is certainly an adventurous and amusing method of travelling, and well worth trying for once in a way; but I am not at all sure that I should enjoy a second experience of it, and I have my doubts on this account, — to say nothing of my dread of a second jolting journey in a Char, — about the propriety of undertaking another journey to Switzerland during the present sultry season. It will be wisest, perhaps, to try the effect of a new scene from the past, representing some former visit to some other locality, before I venture on arriving at a decision. I have rejected Austrian Italy and German Switzerland, and I am doubtful about Switzerland Proper. Suppose I do my duty as a patriot, and give the attractions of my own country a fair chance of appealing to any past influences of the agreeable kind which they may have exercised over me? Black

Mirror! when I was last a tourist at home, how did I travel about from place to place?

The cloud on the magic surface rises slowly and grandly, like the lifting of a fog at sea, and discloses a tiny drawing-room, with a sky-light window, and a rose-colored curtain drawn over it to keep out the sun. A bright book-shelf runs all round this little fairy chamber, just below the ceiling, where the cornice would be in loftier rooms. Sofas extend along the wall on either side, and mahogany cupboards full of good things ensconce themselves snugly in the four corners. The table is brightened with nosegays; the mantel-shelf has a smart railing all round it; and the looking-glass above is just large enough to reflect becomingly the face and shoulders of any lady who will give herself the trouble of looking into it. The present inhabitants of the room are three gentlemen with novels and newspapers in their hands, taking their ease in blouses, dressing-gowns, and slippers. They are reposing on the sofas, with fruit and wine within easy reach; and one of the party looks to me very much like the enviable possessor of the Black Mirror. They exhibit a spectacle of luxury which would make an ancient Spartan shudder with disgust; and, in an adjoining apartment, their band is attending on them, in the shape of a musical box, which is just now playing the last scene in "Lucia di Lammermoor."

Hark! what sounds are those mingling with the notes of Donizetti's lovely music — now rising over it sublimely, now dying away under it, gently and more gently still? Our sweet opera air shall come to its close, our music shall play for its short destined time, and then be silent again; but those more glorious sounds shall go on with us day and night, shall still swell and sink inexhaustibly, long after we and all who know and love and remember us have passed from this earth forever. It is the wash of the waves that now travels along with us grandly wherever we go. We are at sea in a schooner-yacht, and are taking our pleasure along the southern shores of the English coast.

Yes, this to every man who can be certain of his own stomach, this is the true luxury of travelling, the true secret for thoroughly enjoying all the attractions of moving about from place to place. Wherever we now go, we carry our elegant and comfortable home along with us. We can stop where we like, see what we like, and always come back to our favorite corner on the sofa, always carry on our favorite occupations and amusements, and still be travelling, still be getting forward to new scenes all the time. Here is no hurrying to accommodate yourself to other's people's hours for starting, no scrambling for places, no wearisome watchfulness over baggage. Here are no anxieties about strange beds, — for have we not each of us our own sweet little cabin to nestle in at night? — no agitating dependence at the dinner-hour upon the vagaries of strange cooks, — for have we not our own sumptuous larder always to return to, our own accomplished and faithful culinary artist always waiting to minister to our special tastes? We can walk and sleep, stand up or lie down, just as we please, in our floating travel-ling-carriage. We can make our own road, and trespass nowhere. The bores we dread, the letters we don't want to answer, cannot follow and annoy us. We are the freest travellers under heaven; and we find something to in-terest and attract us through every hour of the day. The ships we meet, the trimming of our sails, the varying of the weather, the everlasting innu-merable changes of the ocean, afford constant occupation for eye and ear. Sick, indeed, must that libellous trav-eller have been who first called the sea monotonous — sick to death, and, per-haps, born brother also to that other traveller, of evil renown, the first man who journeyed from Dan to Beersheba, and found all barren.

Rest, then, a while unemployed, my faithful Black Mirror! The last scene you have shown me is sufficient to answer the purpose for which I took you up. Toward what point of the compass I may turn after leaving Lon-don is more than I can tell; but this I know, that my next post-horses shall be the winds, my next stages coast towns, my next road over the open waves. I will be a sea traveller once more, and will put off resuming my land journeyings until the arrival of that most obliging of all convenient periods of time — a future oppor-tunity.

SKETCHES OF CHARACTER.—I.

MRS. BADGERY.

[Drawn from the Life.   By a Gentleman with no Sensibilities.]

Is there any law in England which will protect me from Mrs. Badgery?

I am a bachelor, and Mrs. Badgery is a widow. Don't suppose she wants to marry me! She wants nothing of the sort. · She has not attempted to marry me; she would not think of marrying me, even if I asked her. Understand, if you please, at the outset, that my grievance in relation to this widow lady is a grievance of an entirely new kind.

Let me begin again. I am a bachelor of a certain age. I have a large circle of acquaintance; but I solemnly declare that the late Mr. Badgery was never numbered on the list of my friends. I never heard of him in my life; I never knew that he had left a relict; I never set eyes on Mrs. Badgery until one fatal morning when I went to see if the fixtures were all right in my new house.

My new house is in the suburbs of London. I looked at it, liked it, took it. Three times I visited it before I sent my furniture in. Once with a friend, once with a surveyor, once by myself, to throw a sharp eye, as I have already intimated, over the fixtures. The third visit marked the fatal occasion on which I first saw Mrs. Badgery. A deep interest attaches to this event, and I shall go into details in describing it.

I rang at the bell of the garden door. The old woman appointed to keep the house answered it. I directly saw something strange and confused in her face and manner. Some men would have pondered a little and questioned her. I am by nature impetuous and a rusher at conclusions. "Drunk," I said to myself, and walked on into the house perfectly satisfied.

I looked into the front parlor. Grate all right, curtain-pole all right, gas chandelier all right. I looked into the back parlor — ditto, ditto, ditto, as we men of business say. I mounted the stairs. Blind on back window right? Yes; blind on back window right. I opened the door of the front drawing-room — and there, sitting in the middle of the bare floor, was a large woman on a little camp-stool! She was dressed in the deepest mourning; her face was hidden by the thickest crape veil ever I saw; and she was groaning softly to herself in the desolate solitude of my new unfurnished house.

What did I do? Do! I bounced back into the landing as if I had been shot, uttering the national exclamation of terror and astonishment, " Hullo!" (And here I particularly beg, in parenthesis, that the printer will follow my spelling of the word, and not put Hillo or Halloo instead, both of which are senseless compromises which represent no sound that ever yet issued from an Englishman's lips.) I said, " Hullo!" and then I turned round fiercely upon the old woman who kept the house, and said " Hullo!" again.

She understood the irresistible appeal that I had made to her feelings, and courtesied, and looked toward the drawing-room, and humbly hoped that I was not startled or put out. I asked who the crape-covered woman on the camp-stool was, and what she wanted there. Before the old woman could answer, the soft groaning in the drawing-room ceased, and a muffled voice, speaking from behind the crape veil addressed me reproachfully, and said : —

" I am the widow of the late Mr. Badgery."

What do you think I said in answer? Exactly the words which I flatter myself any other sensible man in my situation would have said. And what words were they? These two : —

" Oh, indeed?"

" Mr. Badgery and myself were the last tenants who inhabited this house," continued the muffled voice. " Mr. Badgery died here." The voice ceased, and the soft groans began again.

It was perhaps unnecessary to answer this ; but I did answer it. How! in two words again : —

" Did he?"

" Our house has been long empty," resumed the voice, choked by sobs. " Our establishment has been broken up. Being left in reduced circumstances, I now live in a cottage near ; but it is not home to me. This is home. However long I live, wherever I go, whatever changes may happen to this beloved house, nothing can ever prevent me from looking on it as my home. I came here, sir, with Mr. Badgery after our honeymoon. All the brief happiness of my life was once contained within these four walls. Every dear remembrance that I fondly cherish is shut up in these sacred rooms."

Again the voice ceased, and again the soft groans echoed round my empty walls, and oozed out past me down my uncarpeted staircase.

I reflected. Mrs. Badgery's brief happiness and dear remembrances were not included in the list of fixtures. Why could she not take them away with her? Why should she leave them littered about in the way of my furniture?

I was just thinking how I could put this view of the case strongly to Mrs. Badgery, when she suddenly left off groaning and addressed me once more.

" While this house has been empty," she said, " I have been in the habit of looking in from time to time, and renewing my tender associations with the place. I have lived, as it were, in the sacred memories of Mr. Badgery and of the past, which these dear, these priceless rooms call up, dismantled and dusty as they are at the present moment. It has been my practice to give a remuneration to the attendant for any slight trouble that I might occasion—"

"Only sixpence, sir," whispered the old woman, close at my ear.

"And to ask nothing in return," continued Mrs. Badgery, "but the permission to bring my camp-stool with me, and to meditate on Mr. Badgery in the empty rooms, with every one of which some happy thought, or eloquent word, or tender action of his, is everlastingly associated. I came here on my usual errand to-day. I am discovered, I presume, by the new proprietor of the house,—discovered, I am quite ready to admit, as an intruder. I am willing to go, if you wish it after hearing my explanation. My heart is full, sir; I am quite incapable of contending with you. You would hardly think it, but I am sitting on the spot once occupied by *our* ottoman. I am looking toward the window in which *my* flower-stand once stood. In this very place Mr. Badgery first sat down and clasped me to his heart, when we came back from our honeymoon trip. 'Matilda,' he said, 'your drawing-room has been expensively papered, carpeted, and furnished for a month; but it has only been adorned, love, since you entered it." If you have no sympathy, sir, for such remembrances as these; if you see nothing pitiable in my position, taken in connection with my presence here; if you cannot enter into my feelings, and thoroughly understand that this is not a house, but a Shrine—you have only to say so, and I am quite willing to go."

She spoke with the air of a martyr, —a martyr to my insensibility. If she had been the proprietor and I had been the intruder, she could not have been more mournfully magnanimous. All this time, too, she has never raised her veil—she never has raised it, in 'my presence, from that time to this. I have no idea whether she is young or old, dark or fair, handsome or ugly; my impression is, that she is in every respect a finished and perfect Gorgon; but I have no basis of fact on which I can support that horrible idea. A moving mass of crape and a muffled voice, —that, if you drive me to it, is all I know, in a personal point of view, of Mrs. Badgery.

"Ever since my irreparable loss, this has been the shrine of my pilgrimage, and the altar of my worship," proceeded the voice. "One man may call himself a landlord, and say that he will let it; another man may call himself a tenant, and say that he will take it. I don't blame either of those two men; I don't wish to intrude on either of those two men; I only tell them that this is my home; that my heart is still in possession, and that no mortal laws, landlords, or tenants can ever turn it out. If you don't understand this, sir; if the holiest feelings that do honor to our common nature have no particular sanctity in your estimation, pray do not scruple to say so; pray tell me to go."

"I don't wish to do anything uncivil, ma'am," said I. "But I am a single man, and I am not sentimental." (Mrs. Badgery groaned.) "Nobody told me I was coming into a Shrine when I took this house; nobody warned me, when I first went over it, that there was a Heart in possession. I regret to have disturbed your meditations, and I am sorry to hear that Mr. Badgery is dead. That is all I have to say about it; and now, with your kind permission, I will do myself the honor of wishing you good-morning, and will go upstairs to look after the fixtures on the second floor."

Could I have given a gentler hint than this? Could I have spoken more compassionately to a woman whom I sincerely believe to be old and ugly? Where is the man to be found who can lay his hand on his heart and honestly say that he ever really pitied the sorrows of a Gorgon? Search through the whole surface of the globe, and you will discover human phenomena of all sorts; but you will not find that man.

To resume. I made her a bow, and left her on the camp-stool in the middle of the drawing-room floor, exactly as I had found her. I ascended to the second floor, walked into the back room first, and inspected the grate. It appeared to be a little out of repair, so I stooped down to look at it closer. While I was kneeling over the bars, I was violently startled by the fall of one large drop of warm water, from a great height, exactly in the middle of a bald place, which has been widening a great deal of late years on the top of my head. I turned on my knees, and looked round. Heaven and earth! the crape-covered woman had followed me upstairs — the source from which the drop of warm water had fallen was Mrs. Badgery's eye!

"I wish you could contrive not to cry over the top of my head, ma'am," I remarked. My patience was becoming exhausted, and I spoke with considerable asperity. The curly-headed youth of the present age may not be able to sympathize with my feelings on this occasion; but my bald brethren know as well as I do that the most unpardonable of all liberties is a liberty taken with the unguarded top of the human head.

Mrs. Badgery did not seem to hear me. When she had dropped the tear, she was standing exactly over me, looking down at the grate; and she never stirred an inch after I had spoken. "Don't cry over my head, ma'am," I repeated, more irritably than before.

"This was his dressing-room," said Mrs. Badgery, indulging in muffled soliloquy. "He was singularly particular about his shaving-water. He always liked to have it in a little tin pot, and he invariably desired that it might be placed on this hob." She groaned again, and tapped one side of the grate with the leg of her camp-stool.

If I had been a woman, or if Mrs. Badgery had been a man, I should now have proceeded to extremities, and should have vindicated my right to my own house by an appeal to physical force. Under existing circumstances, all that I could do was to express my indignation by a glance. The glance produced not the slightest result — and no wonder. Who can look at a woman with any effect through a crape veil?

I retreated into the second-floor front room, and instantly shut the door after me. The next moment I heard the rustling of the crape garments outside, and the muffled voice of Mrs. Badgery poured lamentably through the key-hole.

"Do you mean to make that your bedroom?" asked the voice on the other side of the door. "Oh, don't, don't make that your bedroom! I am going away directly — but, oh pray, pray let that one room be sacred! Don't sleep there! If you can possibly help it, don't sleep there!"

I opened the window, and looked up and down the road. If I had seen a policeman within hail I should certainly have called him in. No such person was visible. I shut the window again, and warned Mrs. Badgery, through the door, in my sternest tones, not to interfere with my domestic arrangements. "I mean to have my own iron bedstead put up here," I said. "And what is more, I mean to sleep here. And what is more, I mean to snore here!" Severe, I think, that last sentence? It completely crushed Mrs. Badgery for the moment. I heard the crape garments rustling away from the door; I heard the muffled groans going slowly and solemnly down the stairs again.

In due course of time I also descended to the ground-floor. Had Mrs. Badgery really left the premises? I looked into the front parlor — empty. Back parlor — empty. Any other room on the ground-floor? Yes; a long room at the end of the passage. The door was closed. I opened it cautiously, and peeped in. A faint scream, and a smack of two distractedly clasped hands saluted my appearance. There she was, again on the camp-stool, again sitting exactly in the middle of the floor.

"Don't, don't look in, in that way!" cried Mrs. Badgery, wringing her hands. "I could bear it in any other room, but I can't bear it in this. Every Monday morning I looked out the things for the wash in this room. He was difficult to please about his linen; the washerwoman never put starch enough into his collars to satisfy him. Oh, how often and often has he popped his head in here, as you popped yours just now, and said, in his amusing way, 'More starch!' Oh, how droll he always was — how very, very droll in this dear little back room!"

I said nothing. The situation had now got beyond words. I stood with the door in my hand, looking down the passage toward the garden, and waiting doggedly for Mrs. Badgery to go out. My plan succeeded. She rose, sighed, shut up the camp-stool, stalked along the passage, paused on the hall mat, said to herself, "Sweet, sweet spot!" descended the steps, groaned along the gravel-walk, and disappeared from view at last through the garden door.

"Let her in again at your peril!" said I to the woman who kept the house. She courtesied and trembled. I left the premises, satisfied with my own conduct under very trying circumstances; delusively convinced also that I had done with Mrs. Badgery.

The next day I sent in the furniture. The most unprotected object on the face of this earth is a house when the furniture is going in. The doors must be kept open; and, employ as many servants as you may, nobody can be depended on as a domestic sentry so long as the van is at the gate. The confusion of "moving in" demoralizes the steadiest disposition, and there is no such thing as a properly guarded post from the top of the house to the bottom. How the invasion was managed, how the surprise was effected, I know not; but it is certainly the fact that, when my furniture went in, the inevitable Mrs. Badgery went in along with it.

I have some very choice engravings, after the old masters; and I was first awakened to a consciousness of Mrs. Badgery's presence in the house while I was hanging up my proof impression of Titian's Venus over the front-parlor fire-place. "Not there!" cried the muffled voice, imploringly. "*His* portrait used to hang there. Oh, what a print — what a dreadful, dreadful print to put where *his* dear portrait used to be!"

I turned round in a fury. There she was, still muffled up in crape, still carrying her abominable camp-stool. Before I could say a word in remonstrance, six men in green baize aprons staggered in with my sideboard, and Mrs. Badgery suddenly disappeared. Had they trampled her under foot, or crushed her in the door-way? Though not an inhuman man by nature, I asked myself those questions quite composedly. No very long time elapsed before they were practically answered in the negative by the reappearance of Mrs. Badgery herself, in a perfectly unruffled condition of chronic grief. In the course of the day I had my toes trodden on, I was knocked about by my own furniture, the six men in baize aprons

dropped all sorts of small articles over me in going up and down stairs; but Mrs. Badgery escaped unscathed. Every time I thought she had been turned out of the house she proved, on the contrary, to be groaning close behind me. She wept over Mr. Badgery's memory in every room, perfectly undisturbed to the last by the chaotic confusion of moving in. I am not sure, but I think she brought a tin box of sandwiches with her, and celebrated a tearful picnic of her own in the groves of my front garden. I say I am not sure of this; but I am positively certain that I never entirely got rid of her all day; and I know to my cost that she insisted on making me as well acquainted with Mr. Badgery's favorite notions and habits as I am with my own. It may interest the reader if I report that my taste in carpets is not equal to Mr. Badgery's; that my ideas on the subject of servants' wages are not so generous as Mr. Badgery's; and that I ignorantly persisted in placing a sofa in the position which Mr. Badgery, in his time, considered to be particularly fitted for an arm-chair. I could go nowhere, look nowhere, do nothing, say nothing, all that day, without bringing the widowed incubus in the crape garments down upon me immediately. I tried civil remonstrances, I tried rude speeches, I tried sulky silence — nothing had the least effect on her. The memory of Mr. Badgery was the shield of proof with which she warded off my fiercest attacks. Not till the last article of furniture had been moved in did I lose sight of her; and even then she had not really left the house. One of my six men in green baize aprons routed her out of the back-garden area, where she was telling my servants, with floods of tears, of Mr. Badgery's virtuous strictness with his house-maid in the matter of followers. My admirable man in green baize courageously saw her out, and shut the garden door after her. I gave him half a crown on the spot; and if anything happens to him, I am ready to make the future prosperity of his fatherless family my own peculiar care.

The next day was Sunday, and I attended morning service at my new parish church.

A popular preacher had been announced, and the building was crowded. I advanced a little way up the nave, and looked to my right, and saw no room. Before I could look to my left, I felt a hand laid persuasively on my arm. I turned round — and there was Mrs. Badgery, with her pew door open, solemnly beckoning me in. The crowd had closed up behind me; the eyes of a dozen members of the congregation, at least, were fixed on me. I had no choice but to save appearances, and accept the dreadful invitation. There was a vacant place next to the door of the pew. I tried to drop into it, but Mrs. Badgery stopped me. "*His* seat," she whispered, and signed to me to place myself on the other side of her. It is unnecessary to say that I had to climb over a hassock, and that I knocked down all Mrs. Badgery's devotional books before I succeeded in passing between her and the front of the pew. She cried uninterruptedly through the service; composed herself when it was over; and began to tell me what Mr. Badgery's opinions had been on points of abstract theology. Fortunately there was great confusion and crowding at the door of the church; and I escaped, at the hazard of my life, by running round the back of the carriages. I passed the interval between the services alone in the fields, being deterred from going home by the fear that Mrs. Badgery might have got there before me.

Monday came. I positively ordered my servants to let no lady in deep mourning pass inside the garden door without first consulting me. After that, feeling tolerably secure, I occupied myself in arranging my books and prints.

I had not pursued this employment much more than an hour, when one of the servants burst excitely into the room and informed me that a lady in deep mourning had been taken faint just outside my door, and had requested leave to come in and sit down for a few moments. I ran down the garden path to bolt the door, and arrived just in time to see it violently pushed open by an officious and sympathizing crowd. They drew away on either side as they saw me. There she was, leaning on the grocer's shoulder, with the butcher's boy in attendance, carrying her campstool! Leaving my servants to do what they liked with her, I ran back and locked myself up in my bedroom. When she evacuated the premises, some hours afterwards, I received a message of apology, informing me that this particular Monday was the sad anniversary of her wedding-day, and that she had been taken faint, in consequence, at the sight of her lost husband's house.

Tuesday forenoon passed away happily, without any new invasion. After lunch I thought I would go out and take a walk. My garden door has a sort of peep-hole in in it, covered with a wire grating. As I got close to this grating, I thought I saw something mysteriously dark on the outer side of it. I bent my head down to look through, and instantly found myself face to face with the crape veil. " Sweet, sweet spot!" said the muffled voice, speaking straight into my eyes through the grating. The usual groans followed, and the name of Mr. Badgery was plaintively pronounced before I could recover myself sufficiently to retreat to the house.

Wednesday is the day on which I am writing this narrative. It is not twelve o'clock yet, and there is every probability that some new form of sentimental persecution is in store for me before the evening. Thus far, these lines contain a perfectly true statement of Mrs. Badgery's conduct toward me since I entered on the possession of *my* house and *her* shrine. What am I to do — that is the point I wish to insist on — what am I to do? How am I to get away from the memory of Mr. Badgery, and the unappeasable grief of his disconsolate widow? Any other species of invasion it is possible to resist; but how is a man placed in my unhappy and unparalleled circumstances to defend himself? I can't keep a dog ready to fly at Mrs. Badgery. I can't charge her at a police court with being oppressively fond of the house in which her husband died. I can't set man-traps for a woman, or prosecute a weeping widow as a trespasser and a nuisance. I am helplessly involved in the unrelaxing folds of Mrs. Badgery's crape veil. Surely there was no exaggeration in my language when I said that I was a sufferer under a perfectly new grievance ! Can anybody advise me? Has anybody had even the remotest experience of the peculiar form of persecution which I am now enduring? If nobody has, is there any legal gentleman in the United Kingdom who can answer the all-important question which appears at the head of this narrative? I began by asking that question because it was uppermost in my mind. It is uppermost in my mind still, and I therefore beg leave to conclude appropriately by asking it again : —

Is there any law in England which will protect me from Mrs. Badgery?

A CASE WORTH LOOKING AT.

MEMOIRS OF AN ADOPTED SON.*

I.— CIRCUMSTANCES WHICH PRECEDED HIS BIRTH.

TOWARD the beginning of the eighteenth century, there stood on a rock in the sea, near a fishing village on the coast of Brittany, a ruined tower with a very bad reputation. No mortal was known to have inhabited it within the memory of living man. The one tenant whom Tradition associated with the occupation of the place at a remote period had moved into it from the infernal regions nobody knew why — had lived in it nobody knew how long.— and had quitted possession nobody knew when. Under such circumstances, nothing was more natural than that this unearthly Individual should give a name to his residence; for which reason, the building was thereafter known to all the neighborhood round as Satanstower.

Early in the year seventeen hundred, the inhabitants of the village were startled one night by seeing the red gleam of a fire in the tower, and by smelling, in the same direction, a preternaturally strong odor of fried fish. The next morning, the fishermen who passed by the building in their boats were amazed to find a stranger had taken up his abode in it. Judging of him at a distance, he seemed to be a fine, tall, stout fellow: he was dressed in fisherman's costume, and he had a new boat of his own, moored comfortably in a cleft of the rock. If he had inhabited a place of decent reputation, his neighbors would have immediately made his acquaintance; but, as things were, all they could venture to do was to watch him in silence.

The first day passed, and, though it was fine weather, he made no use of

---

* The curious legend connected with the birth of this "Adopted Son," and the facts relating to his extraordinary career in after-life, are derived from the "Records" of the French Police of the period. In this instance, and in the instances of those other papers in the present collection, which deal with foreign incidents and characters, while the facts of each narrative exist in print, the form in which the narrative is cast is of my own devising. If these facts had been readily accessible to readers in general, the papers in question would not have been reprinted. But the scarce and curious books from which my materials are derived have been long since out of print, and are, in all human probability, never likely to be published again.

his boat. The second day followed, with a continuance of the fine weather, and still he was as idle as before. On the third day, when a violent storm kept all the boats of the village on the beach, — on the third day, in the midst of the tempest, away went the man of the tower to make his first fishing experiment in strange waters! He and his boat came back safe and sound, in a lull of the storm; and the villagers watching on the cliff above saw him carrying the fish up, by great basketfuls, to his tower. No such haul had ever fallen to the lot of any one of them, and the stranger had taken it in a wild gale of wind.

Upon this the inhabitants of the village called a council. The lead in the debate was assumed by a smart young fellow, a fisherman, named Poulailler, who stoutly declared that the stranger at the tower was of infernal origin. "The rest of you may call him what you like," said Poulailler; "I call him The Fiend-Fisherman!"

The opinion thus expressed proved to be the opinion of the entire audience — with the one exception of the village priest. The priest said, "Gently, my sons. Don't make sure about the man of the tower before Sunday. Wait and see if he comes to church."

"And if he doesn't come to church?" asked all the fishermen, in a breath.

"In that case," replied the priest, "I will excommunicate him; and then, my children, you may call him what you like."

Sunday came, and no sign of the stranger darkened the church doors. He was excommunicated accordingly.

The whole village forthwith adopted Poulailler's idea, and called the man of the tower by the name which Poulailler had given him — "The Fiend-Fisherman."

These strong proceedings produced not the slightest apparent effect on the diabolical personage who had occasioned them. He persisted in remaining idle when the weather was fine, in going out to fish when no other boat in the place dare put to sea, and in coming back again to his solitary dwelling-place with his nets full, his boat uninjured, and himself alive and hearty. He made no attempt to buy and sell with anybody, he kept steadily away from the village, he lived on fish of his own preternaturally strong frying, and he never spoke to a living soul, with the solitary exception of Poulailler himself. One fine evening, when the young man was rowing home past the tower, the Fiend-Fisherman darted out on to the rock, said, "Thank you, Poulailler, for giving me a name," bowed politely, and darted in again. The young fisherman felt the words run cold down the marrow of his back; and whenever he was at sea again, he gave the tower a wide berth from that day forth.

Time went on, and an important event occurred in Poulailler's life. He was engaged to be married. On the day when his betrothal was publicly made known, his friends clustered noisily about him on the fishing-jetty of the village to offer their congratulations. While they were all in full cry, a strange voice suddenly made itself heard through the confusion, which silenced everybody in an instant. The crowd ·fell back, and disclosed the Fiend-Fisherman sauntering up the jetty. It was the first time he had ever set foot — cloven foot — within the precincts of the village.

"Gentlemen," said the Fiend-Fisherman, "where is my friend Poulailler?" He put the question with perfect politeness; he looked remarkably well in his fisherman's costume; he exhaled a relishing odor of fried fish; he had a cordial nod for the men, and a sweet smile for the women; but, with all these personal advantages, everybody fell back from him, and nobody answered his question. The coldness of the popular reception, however, did not in any way abash him. He looked about for Poulailler with searching eyes, discovered the place in which he was standing, and addressed him in the friendliest manner.

"So you are going to be married?" remarked the Fiend-Fisherman.

"What's that to you?" said Poulailler. He was inwardly terrified, but outwardly gruff — not an uncommon combination of circumstances with men of his class in his mental situation.

"My friend," pursued the Fiend-Fisherman, "I have not forgotten your polite attention in giving me a name, and I come here to requite it. You will have a family, Poulailler, and your first child will be a boy. I propose to make that boy my adopted son."

The marrow of Poulailler's back became awfully cold; but he grew gruffer than ever, in spite of his back.

"You won't do anything of the sort," he replied. "If I have the largest family in France, no child of mine shall ever go near you."

"I shall adopt your first-born for all that," persisted the Fiend-Fisherman. "Poulailler, I wish you good-morning. Ladies and gentlemen, the same to all of you."

With those words he withdrew from the jetty, and the marrow of Poulailler's back recovered its temperature.

The next morning was stormy, and all the village expected to see the boat from the tower put out, as usual, to sea. Not a sign of it appeared. Later in the day the rock on which the building stood was examined from a distance. Neither boat nor nets were in their customary places. At night the red gleam of the fire was missed for the first time. The Fiend-Fisherman had gone! He had announced his intentions on the jetty, and had disappeared. What did this mean? Nobody knew.

On Poulailler's wedding-day, a portentous circumstance recalled the memory of the diabolical stranger, and, as a matter of course, seriously discomposed the bridegroom's back. At the moment when the marriage ceremony was complete, a relishing odor of fried fish stole into the nostrils of the company, and a voice from invisible lips said, "Keep up your spirits, Poulailler; I have not forgotten my promise!"

A year later Madame Poulailler was in the hands of the midwife of the district, and a repetition of the portentous circumstance took place. Poulailler was waiting in the kitchen to hear how matters ended upstairs. The nurse came in with a baby. "Which is it?" asked the happy father; "girl or boy?"

Before the nurse could answer, an odor of supernaturally fried fish filled the kitchen, and a voice from invisible lips replied, "A boy, Poulailler, *and I've got him!*"

Such were the circumstances under which the subject of this memoir was introduced to the joys and sorrows of mortal existence.

II. — HIS BOYHOOD AND EARLY LIFE.

When a boy is born under auspices which lead his parents to suppose that, while the bodily part of him is safe at home, the spiritual part is subjected to a course of infernal tuition elsewhere, what are his father and mother to do with him? They must do the best they can,— which was exactly what Poulailler and his wife did with the hero of these pages.

In the first place, they had him christened instantly. It was observed with horror that his infant face was distorted with grimaces, and that his infant voice roared with a preternatural lustiness of tone the moment the priest touched him. The first thing he asked for, when he learned to speak, was "fried fish;" and the first place he wanted to go to, when he learned to walk, was the diabolical tower on the rock. "He won't learn anything," said the master, when he was old enough to go to school. "Thrash him," said Poulailler; and the master thrashed him. "He won't come to his first communion," said the priest. "Thrash him," said Poulailler; and the priest thrashed him. The farmers' orchards were robbed; the neighboring rabbit-warrens were depopulated; linen was stolen from the gardens, and nets were torn on the beach. "The deuce take Poulailler's boy," was the general cry. "The deuce has got him," was Poulailler's answer. "And yet he is a nice-looking boy," said Madame Poulailler. And he was, — as tall, as strong, as handsome a young fellow as could be seen in all France, "Let us pray for him," said Madame Poulailler. "Let us thrash him," said her husband. "Our son has been thrashed till all the sticks in the neighborhood are broken," pleaded his mother. "We will try him with the rope's-end next," retorted his father; "he shall go to sea, and live in an atmosphere of thrashing. Our son shall be a cabin-boy." It was all one to Poulailler Junior; he knew who had adopted him, as well as his father; he had been instinctively conscious from infancy of the Fiend-Fisherman's interest in his welfare; he cared for no earthly discipline; and a cabin-boy he became at ten years old.

After two years of the rope's-end (applied quite ineffectually), the subject of this memoir robbed his captain, and ran away in an English port. London became the next scene of his adventures. At twelve years old he persuaded society in the metropolis that he was the forsaken natural son of a French duke. British benevolence, after blindly providing for him for four years, opened its eyes and found him out at the age of sixteen; upon which he returned to France, and entered the army in the capacity of drummer. At eighteen he deserted, and had a turn with the gypsies. He told fortunes, he conjured, he danced on the tight-rope, he acted, he sold quack medicines, he altered his mind again, and returned to the army. Here he fell in love with the vivandière of his new regiment. The sergeant-major of the company, touched by the same amiable weakness, naturally resented his attentions to the lady. Poulailler (perhaps unjustifiably) asserted himself by boxing his officer's ears. Out flashed the swords on both sides, and in went Poulailler's blade through and through the tender heart of the sergeant-major. The frontier was close at hand. Poulailler wiped his sword, and crossed it.

Sentence of death was recorded against him in his absence. When society has condemned us to die, if we are men of any spirit how are we to return the compliment? By condemning society to keep us alive — or, in other words, by robbing right and left for a living. Poulailler's destiny was now accomplished. He was picked out to be the greatest thief of his age; and when Fate summoned him to his place in the world, he stepped forward and took it. His life hitherto had been merely the life of a young scamp; he was now to do justice to the diabolical father who had adopted him, and to expand to the proportions of a full-grown robber.

His first exploits were performed in Germany. They showed such novelty of combination, such daring, such dexterity, and, even in his most homicidal moments, such irresistible gayety and good humor, that a band of congenial spirits gathered about him in no time. As commander-in-chief of the thieves' army, his popularity never wavered.

His weaknesses — and what illustrious man is without them? — were three in number. First weakness: he was extravagantly susceptible to the charms of the fair sex. Second weakness: he was perilously fond of practical jokes. Third weakness (inherited from his adopted parent): his appetite was insatiable in the matter of fried fish. As for the merits to set against these defects some have been noticed already, and others will appear immediately. Let it merely be premised in this place that he was one of the handsomest men of his time, that he dressed superbly, and that he was capable of the most exalted acts of generosity wherever a handsome woman was concerned; let this be understood, to begin with; and let us now enter on the narrative of his last exploit in Germany before he returned to France. This adventure is something more than a mere specimen of his method of workmanship; it proved, in the future, to be the fatal event of his life.

On a Monday in the week he had stopped on the highway, and robbed of all his valuables and all his papers an Italian nobleman — the Marquis Petrucci, of Sienna. On Tuesday he was ready for another stroke of business. Posted on the top of a steep hill, he watched the road which wound up to the summit on one side, while his followers were ensconced on the road which led down from it on the other. The prize expected in this case was the travelling-carriage (with a large sum of money inside) of the Baron De Kirbergen.

Before long Poulailler discerned the

carriage afar off at the bottom of the hill, and in advance of it, ascending the eminence, two ladies on foot. They were the Baron's daughters — Wilhelmina, a fair beauty; Frederica, a brunette — both lovely, both accomplished, both susceptible, both young. Poulailler sauntered down the hill to meet the fascinating travellers. He looked, bowed, introduced himself, and fell in love with Wilhelmina on the spot. Both the charming girls acknowledged in the most artless manner that confinement to the carriage had given them the fidgets, and that they were walking up the hill to try the remedy of gentle exercise. Poulailler's heart was touched, and Poulailler's generosity to the sex was roused in the nick of time. With a polite apology to the young ladies, he ran back, by a short cut, to the ambush on the other side of the hill in which his men were posted.

"Gentlemen!" cried the generous thief, "in the charming name of Wilhelmina de Kirbergen, I charge you all, let the Baron's carriage pass free." The band was not susceptible; the band demurred. Poulailler knew them. He had appealed to their hearts in vain; he now appealed to their pockets. "Gentlemen!" he resumed, "excuse my momentary misconception of your sentiments. Here is my one-half share of the Marquis Petrucci's property. If I divide it among you, will you let the carriage pass free?" The band knew the value of money, and accepted the terms. Poulailler rushed back up the hill, and arrived at the top just in time to hand the young ladies into the carriage. "Charming man!" said the white Whilhelmina to the brown Frederica, as they drove off. Innocent soul! what would she have said if she had known that her personal attractions had saved her father's property? Was she ever to see the charming man again? Yes; she was to see him the next day — and, more than that, Fate was hereafter to link her fast to the robber's life and the robber's doom.

Confiding the direction of the band to his first lieutenant, Poulailler followed the carriage on horseback, and ascertained the place of the Baron's residence that night.

The next morning, a superbly-dressed stranger knocked at the door. "What name, sir?" said the servant. "The Marquis Petrucci, of Sienna," replied Poulailler. "How are the young ladies after their journey?" The Marquis was shown in, and introduced to the Baron. The Baron was naturally delighted to receive a brother nobleman; Miss Wilhelmina was modestly happy to see the charming man again; Miss Frederica was affectionately pleased on her sister's account. Not being of a disposition to lose time where his affections were concerned, Poulailler expressed his sentiments to the beloved object that evening. The next morning he had an interview with the Baron, at which he produced the papers which proved him to be the Marquis. Nothing could be more satisfactory to the mind of the most anxious parent — the two noblemen embraced. They were still in each other's arms, when a second stranger knocked at the door. "What name, sir?" said the servant. "The Marquis Petrucci, of Sienna," replied the stranger. "Impossible!" said the servant; "his lordship is now in the house." — "Show me in, scoundrel!" cried the visitor. The servant submitted, and the two Marquises stood face to face. Poulailler's composure was not shaken in the least; he had come first to the house, and he had got the papers. "You are the villain who robbed me!" cried the true Petrucci. "You are drunk, mad, or an impostor," retorted the false Petrucci. "Send to Florence, where I am known," exclaimed one of the Marquises, apostrophizing the Baron. "Send to Florence by all means," echoed the other, addressing himself to the Baron also. "Gentlemen," replied the noble Kirbergen, "I will do myself the honor of taking your advice" — and he sent to Florence accordingly.

Before the messenger had advanced ten miles on his journey, Poulailler had said two words in private to the susceptible Wilhelmina, and the pair eloped from the baronial residence that night. Once more the subject of this memoir crossed the frontier, and re-entered France. Indifferent to the attractions of rural life, he forthwith established himself with the beloved Wilhelmina in Paris. In that fine city he met with his strangest adventures, performed his boldest achievements, committed his most prodigious robberies, and, in a word, did himself and his infernal patron the fullest justice in the character of the Fiend-Fisherman's adopted son.

III.—HIS CAREER IN PARIS.

Once established in the French metropolis, Poulailler planned and executed that vast system of perpetual robbery and occasional homicide which made him the terror and astonishment of all Paris. In-doors as well as out his good fortune befriended him. No domestic anxieties harassed his mind, and diverted him from the pursuit of his distinguished public career. The attachment of the charming creature with whom he had eloped from Germany survived the discovery that the Marquis Petrucci was Poulailler the robber. True to the man of her choice, the devoted Wilhelmina shared his fortunes, and kept his house. And why not, if she loved him — in the all-conquering name of Cupid, why not?

Joined by picked men from his German followers, and by new recruits gathered together in Paris, Poulailler now set society and its safeguards at flat defiance. Cartouche himself was his inferior in audacity and cunning. In course of time, the whole city was panic-stricken by the new robber and his band — the very boulevards were deserted after night-fall. Monsieur Hérault, lieutenant of police of the period, in despair of laying hands on Poulailler by any other means, at last offered a reward of a hundred pistoles and a place in his office worth two thousand livres a year to any one who would apprehend the robber alive. The bills were posted all over Paris, and the next morning they produced the very last result in the world which the lieutenant of police could possibly have anticipated.

While Monsieur Hérault was at breakfast in his study, the Count De Villeneuve was announced as wishing to speak to him. Knowing the Count by name only, as belonging to an ancient family in Provence or in Languedoc, Monsieur Hérault ordered him to be shown in. A perfect gentleman appeared, dressed with an admirable mixture of magnificence and good taste. "I have something for your private ear, sir," said the Count. "Will you give orders that no one must be allowed to disturb us?"

Monsieur Hérault gave the orders.

"May I inquire, Count, what your business is?" he asked, when the door was closed.

"To earn the reward you offer for taking Poulailler," answered the Count. "I am Poulailler."

Before Monsieur Hérault could open his lips, the robber produced a pretty little dagger and some rose-colored silk cord "The point of this little dagger is poisoned," he observed; "and one scratch of it, my dear sir, would be the death of you." With these words Poulailler gagged the lieutenant of police, bound him to his chair with the rose-colored cord, and lightened his writing-desk of one thousand pistoles. "I'll take money, instead of taking the place in the office which you kindly offer," said Poulailler. "Don't trouble yourself to see me to the door. Good-morning."

A few weeks later, while Monsieur Hérault was still the popular subject of ridicule throughout Paris, business took Poulailler on the road to Lille and Cambrai. The only inside passenger in the coach besides himself was the venerable Dean Potter, of Brussels. They fell into talk on the one interesting subject of the time, — not the weather, but Poulailler.

"It's a disgrace, sir, to the police," said the Dean, "that such a miscreant is still at large. I shall be returning to Paris by this road in ten days' time, and I shall call on Monsieur Hérault to suggest a plan of my own for catching the scoundrel."

"May I ask what it is?" said Poulailler.

"Excuse me," replied the Dean; "you are a stranger, sir, and moreover I wish to keep the merit of suggesting the plan to myself."

"Do you think the lieutenant of police will see you?" asked Poulailler; "he is not accessible to strangers, since the miscreant you speak of played him that trick at his own breakfast-table."

"He will see Dean Potter, of Brussels," was the reply, delivered with the slightest possible tinge of offended dignity.

"Oh, unquestionably!" said Poulailler; "pray pardon me."

"Willingly, sir," said the Dean; and the conversation flowed into other channels.

Nine days later the wounded pride of Monsieur Hérault was soothed by a very remarkable letter. It was signed by one of Poulailler's band, who offered himself as king's evidence, in the hope of obtaining a pardon. The letter stated that the venerable Dean Potter had been waylaid and murdered by Poulailler, and that the robber, with his customary audacity, was about to re-enter Paris by the Lisle coach the next day, disguised in the Dean's own clothes, and furnished with the Dean's own papers. Monsieur

Hérault took his precautions without losing a moment. Picked men were stationed, with their orders, at the barrier through which the coach must pass to enter Paris, while the lieutenant of police waited at his office, in the company of two French gentlemen who could speak to the Dean's identity, in the event of Poulailler's impudently persisting in the assumption of his victim's name.

At the appointed hour the coach appeared, and out of it got a man in the Dean's costume. He was arrested in spite of his protestations ; the papers of the murdered Potter were found on him, and he was dragged off to the police-office in triumph. The door opened, and the *posse comitatus* entered with the prisoner. Instantly the two witnesses burst out with a cry of recognition, and turned indignantly on the lieutenant of police. "Gracious Heaven, sir, what have you done?" they exclaimed in horror ; "this is not Poulailler — here is our venerable friend ; here is the Dean himself!" At the same moment a servant entered with the letter : "Dean Potter. To the care of Monsieur Hérault, Lieutenant of Police." The letter was expressed in these words : "Venerable Sir, — Profit by the lesson I have given you. Be a Christian for the future, and never again try to injure a man unless he tries to injure you. Entirely yours — Poulailler."

These feats of cool audacity were matched by others, in which his generosity to the sex asserted itself as magnanimously as ever.

Hearing one day that large sums of money were kept in the house of a great lady, one Madame De Brienne, whose door was guarded, in anticipation of a visit from the famous thief, by a porter of approved trustworthiness and courage, Poulailler undertook to rob her in spite of her precautions, and succeeded. With a stout pair of leather straps and buckles in his pocket, and with two of his band disguised as a coachman and a footman, he followed Madame De Brienne one night to the theatre. Just before the close of the performance, the lady's coachman and footman were tempted away for five minutes by Poulailler's disguised subordinates to have a glass of wine. No attempt was made to detain them, or to drug their liquor. But in their absence Poulailler had slipped under the carriage, had hung his leather straps round the pole — one to hold by, and one to support his feet — and, with these simple preparations, was now ready to wait for events. Madame De Brienne entered the carriage — the footman got up behind — Poulailler hung himself horizontally under the pole, and was driven home with them under those singular circumstances. He was strong enough to keep his position after the carriage had been taken into the coach-house, and he only left it when the doors were locked for the night. Provided with food beforehand, he waited patiently, hidden in the coach-house, for two days and nights, watching his opportunity of getting into Madame De Brienne's boudoir.

On the third night the lady went to a grand ball ; the servants relaxed in their vigilance while her back was turned, and Poulailler slipped into the room. He found two thousand louisd'ors, which was nothing like the sum he expected, and a pocket-book, which he took away with him to open at home. It contained some stock warrants for a comparatively trifling amount. Poulailler was far too well off to care about taking them, and far too polite, where a lady was concerned, not to send them back again, under those circumstances. Accordingly, Madame de Brienne received her warrants, with a note of apology from the polite thief.

" Pray excuse my visit to your charming boudoir," wrote Poulailler, " in consideration of the false reports of your wealth, which alone induced me to enter it. If I had known what your pecuniary circumstances really were, on the honor of a gentleman, madame, I should have been incapable of robbing you. I cannot return your two thousand louis-d'ors by post, as I return your warrants. But if you are at all pressed for money in future, I shall be proud to assist so distinguished a lady by lending her, from my own ample resources, double the sum of which I regret to have deprived her on the present occasion." This letter was shown to royalty at Versailles. It excited the highest admiration of the court — especially of the ladies. Whenever the robber's name was mentioned, they indulgently referred to him as the Chevalier de Poulailler. Ah! that was the age of politeness, when good-breeding was recognized, even in a thief. Under similar circumstances, who would recognize it now? O tempora! O mores!

On another occasion Poulailler was out one night taking the air, and watching his opportunities on the roofs of the houses, a member of the band being posted in the street below to assist him in case of necessity. While in. this position, sobs and ·groans proceeding from an open back-garret window caught his ear. A parapet rose before the window, which enabled him to climb down and look in. Starving children surrounding a helpless mother, and clamoring for food, was the picture that met his eye. The mother was young and beautiful, and Poulailler's hand impulsively clutched his purse, as a necessary consequence. Before the charitable thief could enter by the window, a man rushed in by the door with a face of horror, and cast a handful of gold into the lovely mother's lap. " My honor is gone," he cried, " but our children are saved! Listen to the circumstances. I met a man in the street below; he was tall and thin; he had a green patch over one eye; he was looking up suspiciously at this house, apparently waiting for somebody. I thought of you — I thought of the children — I seized the suspicious stranger by the collar. Terror overwhelmed him on the spot. 'Take my watch, my money, and my two valuable gold snuff-boxes,' he said, ' but spare my life.' I took them." — " Noble-hearted man! " cried Poulailler, appearing at the window. The husband started; the wife screamed; the children hid themselves. " Let me entreat you to be composed," continued Poulailler. " Sir! I enter on the scene for the purpose of soothing your uneasy conscience. From your vivid description, I recognize the man whose property is now in your wife's lap. Resume your mental tranquillity. You have robbed a robber — in other words vindicated society. Accept my congratulations on your restored innocence. The miserable coward whose collar you seized is one of Poulailler's band. He has lost his stolen property as the fit punishment for his disgraceful want of spirit."

"Who are you?" exclaimed the husband.

"I am Poulailler," replied the illustrious man, with the simplicity of an ancient hero. "Take this purse, and set up in business with the contents. There is a prejudice, sir, in favor of honesty. Give that prejudice a chance. There was a time when I felt it myself; I regret to feel it no longer. Under all varieties of misfortune, an honest man has his consolation still left. Where is it left? Here!" He struck his heart, and the family fell on their knees before him.

"Benefactor of your species!" cried the husband; "how can I show my gratitude?"

"You can permit me to kiss the hand of madame," answered Poulailler.

Madame started to her feet, and embraced the generous stranger. "What more can I do?" exclaimed this lovely woman, eagerly; "O heavens! what more?"

"You can beg your husband to light me downstairs," replied Poulailler. He spoke, pressed their hands, dropped a generous tear, and departed. At that touching moment his own adopted father would not have known him.

This last anecdote closes the record of Poulailler's career in Paris. The lighter and more agreeable aspects of that career have hitherto been design-edly presented, in discreet remembrance of the contrast which the tragic side of the picture must now present. Comedy and Sentiment, twin sisters of French extraction, farewell! Horror enters next on the stage, and enters welcome, in the name of the Fiend-Fisherman's adopted son.

IV. — HIS EXIT FROM THE SCENE.

The nature of Poulailler's more serious achievements in the art of robbery may be realized by reference to one terrible fact. In the police records of the period, more than one hundred and fifty men and women are reckoned up as having met their deaths at the hands of Poulailler and his band. It was not the practice of this formidable robber to take life as well as property, unless life happened to stand directly in his way — in which case he immediately swept off the obstacle without hesitation and without remorse. His deadly determination to rob, which was thus felt by the population in general, was matched by his deadly determination to be obeyed, which was felt by his followers in particular. One of their number, for example, having withdrawn from his allegiance, and having afterward attempted to betray his leader, was tracked to his hiding-place in a cellar, and was there walled up alive in Poulailler's presence, the robber composing the unfortunate wretch's epitaph, and scratching it on the wet plaster with his own hand. Years afterward the inscription was noticed when the house fell into the possession of a new tenant, and was supposed to be nothing more than one of the many jests which the famous robber had practised in his time. When the plaster was removed, the skeleton fell out, and testified that Poulailler was in earnest.

To attempt the arrest of such a man as this by tampering with his followers was practically impossible. No sum of money that could be offered would induce any one of the members of his band to risk the fatal chance of his vengeance. Other means of getting possession of him had been tried, and tried in vain. Five times over the police had succeeded in tracking him to different hiding-places; and on all five occasions, the women — who adored him for his gallantry, his generosity, and his good looks — had helped him to escape. If he had not unconsciously paved the way to his own capture, first by eloping with Mademoiselle Wilhelmina de Kirbergen, and secondly by maltreating her, it is more than doubtful whether the long arm of the law would ever have reached far enough to fasten its grasp on him. As it was, the extremes of love and hatred met at last in the bosom of the devoted Wilhelmina, and the vengeance of a neglected woman accomplished what the whole police force of Paris had been powerless to achieve.

Poulailler, never famous for the constancy of his attachments, had wearied, at an early period, of the companion of his flight from Germany; but Wilhelmina was one of those women whose affections, once aroused, will not take No for an answer. She persisted in attaching herself to a man who had ceased to love her. Poulailler's patience became exhausted; he tried twice to rid himself of his unhappy mistress — once by the knife, and once by poison — and failed on both occasions. For the third and last time, by way of attempting an experiment, of another kind, he established a rival, to drive the German woman out of the house. From that moment his fate was sealed. Maddened by jealous rage, Wilhelmina cast the last fragments of her fondness to the winds. She secretly communicated with the police, and Poulailler met his doom.

A night was appointed with the authorities, and the robber was invited by his discarded mistress to a farewell interview. His contemptuous confidence in her fidelity rendered him careless of his customary precautions. He accepted the appointment, and the two supped together, on the understanding that they were henceforth to be friends and nothing more. Toward the close of the meal Poulailler was startled by a ghastly change in the face of his companion.

"What is wrong with you?" he asked.

"A mere trifle," she answered, looking at her glass of wine. "I can't help loving you still, badly as you have treated me. You are a dead man, Poulailler, and I shall not survive you."

The robber started to his feet, and seized a knife on the table.

"You have poisoned me!" he exclaimed.

"No," she replied. "Poison is my vengeance on myself; and not my vengeance on *you*. You will rise from this table as you sat down to it. But your evening will be finished in prison, and your life will be ended on the wheel."

As she spoke the words, the door was burst open by the police and Poulailler was secured. The same night the poison did its fatal work, and his mistress made atonement with her life for the first, last act of treachery which had revenged her on the man she loved.

Once safely lodged in the hands of justice, the robber tried to gain time to escape in, by promising to make important disclosures. The manœuvre availed him nothing. In those days the Laws of the Land had not yet made acquaintance with the Laws of Humanity. Poulailler was put to the torture — was suffered to recover — was publicly broken on the wheel — and was taken off it alive, to be cast into a blazing fire. By those murderous means Society rid itself of a murderous man, and the idlers on the Boulevards took their evening stroll again in recovered security.

*   *   *   *   *   *

Paris had seen the execution of Poulailler; but if legends are to be trusted, our old friends, the people of the fishing village in Brittany, saw the end of him afterward. On the day and hour when he perished, the heavens darkened; and a terrible storm arose. Once more, and for a moment only, the gleam of the unearthly fire reddened the windows of the old tower. Thunder pealed, and struck the building into fragments. Lightning flashed incessantly over the ruins; and, in the scorching glare of it, the boat which, in former years, had put off to sea whenever the storm rose highest, was seen to shoot out into the raging ocean from the cleft in the rock, and was discovered on this final occasion to be doubly manned. The Fiend-Fisherman sat at the helm; his adopted son tugged at the oars; and a clamor of diabolical voices, roaring loudly and awfully through the storm, wished the pair of them a prosperous voyage.

THE END.

www.ingramcontent.com/pod-product-compliance
Lightning Source LLC
Chambersburg PA
CBHW020411030726
47496CB00007B/2407